PRAISE FOR ANNA CAMPBELL

"*The Seduction of Lord Stone* is romantic, emotional, sexy and funny. In fact, everything I have come to expect from Anna Campbell. I'm looking forward to reading the other Dashing Widows' stories." —*RakesandRascals.com*

"With her marvelous combination of humor and poignancy Anna Campbell writes in such a way that every story of hers has a special meaning and remains like a sentimental keepsake with those fortunate enough to read her work!" —*JeneratedReviews.com*

"*Lord Garson's Bride* is a well written and passionate story that touched my heart and sent my emotions on a rollercoaster ride. I particularly recommend this book for fans of convenient marriages, and those who enjoy seeing a deserving character find out that love is lovelier the second time around." —*Roses Are Blue Reviews*

"Campbell immediately hooks readers, then deftly reels them in with a spellbinding love story fueled by an addictive mixture of sharp wit, lush sensuality, and a wealth of well-delineated characters."—*Booklist, starred review, on A Scoundrel by Moonlight*

"With its superbly nuanced characters, impeccably crafted historical setting, and graceful writing shot through with scintillating wit, Campbell's latest lusciously sensual, flawlessly written historical Regency ... will have romance readers sighing happily with satisfaction."—*Booklist, Starred Review, on What a Duke Dares*

"Campbell makes the Regency period pop in the appealing third Sons of Sin novel. Romantic fireworks, the constraints of custom, and witty banter are combined in this sweet and successful story."—*Publishers Weekly on What a Duke Dares*

"Campbell is exceptionally talented, especially with plots that challenge the reader, and emotions and characters that are complex and memorable."—*Sarah Wendell, Smart Bitches Trashy Books, on A Rake's Midnight Kiss*

"A lovely, lovely book that will touch your heart and remind you why you read romance."—*Liz Carlyle, New York Times bestselling author on What a Duke Dares*

"Campbell holds readers captive with her highly intense, emotional, sizzling and dark romances. She instinctually knows how to play on her readers' fantasies to create a romantic, deep-sigh tale."—*RT Book Reviews, Top Pick, on Captive of Sin*

"Don't miss this novel - it speaks to the wild drama of the heart, creating a love story that really does transcend class."—*Eloisa James, New York Times bestselling author, on Tempt the Devil*

"*Seven Nights in A Rogue's Bed* is a lush, sensuous treat. I was enthralled from the first page to the last and still wanted more."—*Laura Lee Guhrke, New York Times bestselling author*

"No one does lovely, dark romance or lovely, dark heroes like Anna Campbell. I love her books."—*Sarah MacLean, New York Times bestselling author*

"It isn't just the sensuality she weaves into her story that makes Campbell a fan favorite, it's also her strong, three-dimensional characters, sharp dialogue and deft plotting. Campbell intuitively knows how to balance the key elements of the genre and give readers an irresistible, memorable read."—*RT Book Reviews, Top Pick, on Midnight's Wild Passion*

"Anna Campbell is an amazing, daring new voice in romance."—*Lorraine Heath, New York Times bestselling author*

"Ms. Campbell's gorgeous writing a true thing of beauty..."—*Joyfully Reviewed*

"She's the mistress of dark, sexy and brooding and takes us into the dens of iniquity with humor and class."—*Bookseller-Publisher Australia*

"Anna Campbell is a master at drawing a reader in from the very first page and keeping them captivated the whole book through. Ms. Campbell's books are all on my keeper shelf and *Midnight's Wild Passion* will join them proudly. *Midnight's Wild Passion* is a smoothly sensual delight that was a joy to read and I cannot wait to revisit Antonia and Nicholas's romance again."—*Joyfully Reviewed*

"Ms. Campbell gives us...the steamy sex scenes, a heroine whose backbone is pure steel and a stupendous tale of lust and love and you too cannot help but fall in love with this tantalizing novel."—*Coffee Time Romance*

"Anna Campbell offers us again, a lush, intimate, seductive read. I am in awe of the way she keeps the focus tight on the hero and heroine, almost achingly so. Nothing else really exists in this world, but the two main characters. Intimate, sensual story with a hero that will take your breath away."—*Historical Romance Books & More*

ALSO BY ANNA CAMPBELL

Claiming the Courtesan

Untouched

Tempt the Devil

Captive of Sin

My Reckless Surrender

Midnight's Wild Passion

The Sons of Sin series:

Seven Nights in a Rogue's Bed

Days of Rakes and Roses

A Rake's Midnight Kiss

What a Duke Dares

A Scoundrel by Moonlight

Three Proposals and a Scandal

The Dashing Widows:

The Seduction of Lord Stone

Tempting Mr. Townsend

Winning Lord West

Pursuing Lord Pascal

Charming Sir Charles

Catching Captain Nash

Lord Garson's Bride

The Lairds Most Likely:

The Laird's Willful Lass

The Laird's Christmas Kiss

The Highlander's Lost Lady

Christmas Stories:

The Winter Wife

Her Christmas Earl

A Pirate for Christmas

Mistletoe and the Major

A Match Made in Mistletoe

The Christmas Stranger

Other Books:

These Haunted Hearts

Stranded with the Scottish Earl

TEMPTING MR TOWNSEND

THE DASHING WIDOWS BOOK 2

ANNA CAMPBELL

ISBN: 978-0-6483987-4-5

Cover design: By Hang Le

Print editions published by Serenade Publishing
www.serenadepublishing.com

Thanks to my three troupers, Annie, Vanessa and Christine.
I couldn't do this without you.

CHAPTER ONE

Curzon Street, Mayfair, November 1820

"What the devil have you done with my ward, madam?"

Shocked, Fenella jerked her attention from the embroidery that she'd picked up to while away a rare quiet night at home.

Good heavens. A man the size of a mountain had invaded her drawing room.

An angry mountain.

Astonishment, rather than fear, was her immediate reaction. She slid her tambour frame onto the table beside her and straightened in her chair. "And who on earth are you?"

Greaves, her butler, rushed in with two brawny

footmen looming behind him. "My lady, this fellow pushed his way into the house before I could stop him."

The *fellow* clenched his huge fists at his sides and shot her servants a narrow-eyed glare. Despite their size, Tom and John faltered back.

Fenella could see why. The mysterious intruder looked ready to commit murder. Ready, and more than capable. His excellent tailoring did nothing to hide his impressive muscles and the breadth of shoulders and chest.

When he focused that searing stare on her, her stomach jumped with nerves. Was this some madman escaped from confinement? Although he didn't look unhinged. Just furious.

"Don't pretend you don't know who I am," the man said tersely, a northern accent edging his deep, resonant voice. "Just stop all this blasted nonsense and take me to the lad."

Fenella snatched a shallow breath and rose with an appearance of calm. Nobody needed to know about the quaking knees beneath her frothy lemon skirts.

"It isn't nonsense to expect a guest in my house to show some manners," she said evenly. She gestured to a brocade chair, ignoring Greaves's surprise at the way she faced the man down. She was heartily sick of people treating her as if she was too fragile for this rough world. "Pray calm yourself, sir, and state your business. Preferably without blasting and deviling your way through the explanation."

She waited for the intruder to explode into a rage, but he sucked in a deep breath and directed a doubtful glance at the chair. She couldn't blame him. It looked inadequate for his weight. He was all height and brawn, and he turned her airy drawing room into a salon from a doll's house.

"Tom and John, you may go."

"My lady!" Greaves protested as the footmen departed, although not before directing a questioning glance at the butler. "He could be dangerous."

Fenella subjected the stranger to a comprehensive inspection and shook her head. He'd hold his own in a fight, but some powerful instinct told her she was safe from harm. She couldn't say the same for her servants if they attempted to eject him before he'd achieved his purpose, whatever it was. "I don't think so. There's clearly been some mistake."

"Mistake be damned. Please, for God's sake, just tell me Carey is all right."

Carey? A spark of memory stirred in Fenella's mind. Her son Brandon's recent letters had brimmed with praises for a new boy who had quickly become his best friend. "Carey Townsend?"

"Who the dev..." The large man cast her a darkling glance and ran his hand through his windswept coal-black hair. "Of course Carey Townsend, unless your house is packed to the rafters with runaways."

"Carey's not at Eton?" she asked faintly. A horrible premonition gripped her that her son might be in grave trouble. After all, if Brand hadn't run off, too, why would this man expect his ward to be here?

"No, by God. The boys have been missing since early afternoon."

"Boys?" Dear heaven, she'd been right. Sick fear, worse by far than any doubt about the man's intentions, cramped her belly. In the five years since her husband Henry's death at Waterloo, this was the worst crisis she'd faced. Her knees gave up, and she collapsed into her chair. "Brand's with him?"

"Aye."

"Mr…Townsend?" When he nodded to confirm her guess at his name, she went on, "Please, for pity's sake, stop talking in riddles and tell me what's happened."

"So the lads aren't here?" His impatience vibrated like an earthquake, but at least he moderated his roar to a cranky rumble. As he sat, the chair creaked ominously. "Or are you blethering to put me off?"

"If your ward was here, I'd tell you." Her voice shook, and terror knotted her stomach. "But this is the first I've heard of anything wrong."

He frowned. "Your son is a bad influence."

"I doubt that very much, sir." Automatically she defended Brand, while her imagination took flight in hellish directions. The idea of two eleven-year-old boys lost somewhere between Eton and London turned her blood to ice. "If Brandon has done something silly, I place the blame firmly with your—"

"Nephew," the man snarled. "And they've been more

than silly, madam. They've been wantonly irresponsible. Are you sure they're not here?"

She shook her head. "No."

Mr. Townsend's dark eyes regarded her searchingly, then his aggression drained away. "Hell. I was convinced they'd make for your house, but now I see you had no warning of this harebrained prank either. When the boys' housemaster told me that Brand was dying to introduce his new best friend to his mamma, this seemed the logical destination. Especially with Carey missing his own mother."

Through her agitation, she barely heard him. Dread rose to choke her. "We have to find them."

She surged to her feet, then wished she hadn't when the room reeled alarmingly. Out of the corner of her eye, she saw Greaves move to catch her, but Mr. Townsend was too quick.

As his arm curled around her waist, she sank into all-encompassing masculinity. For one lost moment, she drew strength from that bear-like embrace. She was so upset, she could almost forgive his rudeness if he folded her close and told her that all this was just a horrid joke.

"Oh, curse me for a right impulsive fool. I'm sorry, lass." Through the fog in her mind, she was vaguely aware that he didn't sound angry anymore. Instead he sounded kind and concerned. And the Yorkshire accent was remarkably soothing now that he'd stopped shouting. "I shouldn't have blurted the news out like that, but after talking to the school, I assumed I'd find them safe and sound under your protection."

Fenella blinked fiercely to bring the room into focus and told herself to be strong. She couldn't fall into a hysterical heap. Brand needed her. She made a feeble attempt to push free. "Please...please let me go."

"Can you stand up?" Deep-set, disconcertingly perceptive eyes studied her. "You were close to collapsing."

"Well, I'm perfectly steady now," she snapped, irritation reviving her spirit.

"Very well," he said gruffly, but his huge hands lowered her into the chair with surprising care. Given his earlier behaviour, she'd expect him to drop her like a stone. He inspected her briefly before, apparently satisfied with what he saw, he turned to Greaves. "Brandy for her ladyship. She's had a shock."

Thanks to you, she wanted to retort, but restrained herself. She didn't want to risk another outburst. They didn't have time to bicker. They had to find Brand and Carey. With an unsteady hand, she took the glass from Greaves and strove to come up with a coherent plan.

"I'm sorry for shoving my way in here—I thought you were part of some ridiculous scheme to keep Carey from me. The lad's never settled to having me as his guardian." With a sigh, Mr. Townsend subsided into his chair and spoke almost like a reasonable man. At least the china on the mantelpiece stopped rattling.

"I've been worried sick ever since I found out Carey and Brandon had gone."

Fenella struggled against the urge to shriek and run in panicked circles. She needed more information, and at the moment, the domineering Mr. Townsend was her only source. Inhaling to calm rioting nerves, she made her first proper assessment of the man sprawling opposite her. Despite first impressions, he wasn't by any means a yokel. He was dressed in the height of fashion, and the grand surroundings didn't appear to overawe him.

He remained eye-poppingly large. Well over six feet and built like a prizefighter, he was all solid muscle. She thought of a Clydesdale. No, something more predatory and fast-moving. An oversized panther, perhaps.

While not handsome by society's standards, his square-cut features and glittering eyes expressed vigor and determination enough to conquer the world. His nose had been broken at some stage, and his jaw looked to be chiseled from granite.

He was far and away the most daunting creature she'd ever encountered.

Still, that rugged face was strangely fascinating. It was a wrench to look away toward Greaves. Whatever happened next, she'd shared enough private business with the servants for one night. "That will be all, Greaves."

Her butler warily eyed Mr. Townsend. "It might be prudent if I stay, my lady."

Mr. Townsend was at least thirty years younger and a good four stone heavier than her butler. Although she appreciated Greaves's gallantry, Fenella's voice firmed. "I believe our visitor has forsaken his impulse to violence."

As she'd intended, her remark brought a pink tinge to Townsend's tan. Heavens above, he looked like he'd spent his life baking under a tropical sun somewhere out in Sumatra or the Cape Colony.

Once they were alone, Fenella folded trembling hands in her lap. She battened her fear for Brandon deep down inside her and set out to wrest control of this meeting from her visitor. She might want to scream and weep, but she was her son's only help. After five lonely years of widowhood, that role was familiar enough to be second nature. "Tell me everything."

"I became my nephew's guardian about six months ago." To her relief, Mr. Townsend had calmed considerably. "My brother William and his wife Jenny drowned in a yachting accident last summer."

Henry's death had made her tragically familiar with grief. She heard the unspoken pain behind Mr. Townsend's prosaic explanation. "I'm sorry."

"Thank you. I was in Canton at the time."

Fenella hadn't been wrong about his travels. "Canton?"

"The family runs a trading concern. You've probably heard of us."

With a shock, she realized that he must be part of Townsend and Co. In fact, something about his air of command led her to guess that he *was* Townsend and Co. "You're Anthony Townsend?"

Even in aristocratic circles, Anthony Townsend's enormous fortune aroused envy. If she wasn't in such a spin about Brandon, she'd have made the connection earlier. The Townsend trading empire spanned the globe and influenced the destiny of nations.

He frowned. "Didn't you know?"

"You neglected to introduce yourself, sir."

Another faint flush. In circumstances less dire, she'd almost enjoy putting this arrogant creature to the blush.

"I beg your pardon. Again." He leaned forward, dangling big hands between thighs like tree trunks. The chair squeaked in protest at the movement. Good Lord, he was a giant. "I assumed you'd made the connection when you talked about Carey. You clearly know my nephew."

"Only that he's the sportingest cove ever born and a right royal fine fellow. My son didn't consider his family of any importance." Despite herself, she smiled fondly. She was happy that her son made such a good friend—or at least she had been, until Carey Townsend persuaded Brand into this rash escapade.

Mr. Townsend sighed again. "That's pleasing to

hear. I like to think the lad has some spirit—although today's madness hints at a little too much. I hardly know Carey. I'm away so much, and he's always completely tongue-tied in my presence."

"You probably scare the life out of him," Fenella said before she thought better of it.

To her dismay, he whitened, and she realized that her careless remark had stung. Mr. Townsend looked like a flying cannonball would leave no mark, but she came to suspect that a man of genuine feeling lurked beneath all that brusque self-confidence. The hint of vulnerability made her like him better, and she forgave his unconventional entrance. After all, he'd had more than twenty miles from Eton to London to imagine disasters.

"I deserved that," he said quietly. "But whatever Carey thinks of me, I can't leave the lad to wander around on his own, prey to every villain in the land."

She spread her hands, struggling through alarm to make sense of events. "Are you certain the boys are missing? Surely if the school contacted you, they'd contact me. Perhaps Brand and Carey are up to mischief—hiding to cause trouble."

"I'm certain they're missing." Looking deathly tired, Mr. Townsend rubbed one massive hand over his face. "The headmaster left it to me to tell you, although I imagine a letter is on its way. He suggested I come straight here, while they search the local area. I was so quick to find out the boys had gone because I was on the spot. I got into port from Copenhagen this morning and decided to call on the lad and see how he was faring. Thank God I did. Otherwise they'd be gone who knows how long before anyone noticed, damned muddleheaded numbskulls at that school. I should have guessed I was on a wild goose chase, whatever his housemaster's ideas. I asked all along the way, and nobody had seen them."

An agonizing mixture of worry and anger squeezed Fenella's chest. "I could wring Brand's neck." She moderated her tone. Recriminations would do no good. "But to be fair, it's not like him. He's levelheaded, mature beyond his years. This is the most trouble he's ever caused."

Since his father's death, Brandon had been touchingly protective of his mother. It was as if, even at six, he'd taken on Henry's mantle as man of the house.

Mr. Townsend sent her a sharp-eyed glance. "Are you saying it's Carey's fault?"

"I'm saying that there's no use speculating on their reasons at this stage."

"I'd say there's every use. If we knew why they ran away, we can guess where they went." He stood with sudden dispatch and started to pace, his long legs covering the distance from wall to wall in a few strides. Until now, this room had never felt small. With Mr. Townsend quartering the carpet, it became suffocating. "Damn it, there's no point sitting around here. I'll head back to Eton to check the roads leading out of town.

The school's searching across to Windsor, but I've got a feeling the boys are long gone." He fixed those blazing dark eyes on her. "What about the family seat? Would Brandon go there?"

"He might," she said doubtfully. "But I don't see why. He hasn't been there since Henry died, and the place is tenanted with strangers. Where did Carey and his parents live?"

"In Liverpool. William managed our Atlantic shipping from the docks there. But their house was sold after the accident."

"Would he go looking for you?"

"I doubt it," he said grimly. "But I've sent messages to all my offices to be on the lookout just in case."

"Is there anywhere else Carey's likely to go?"

Mr. Townsend growled with frustration. "Hell, I don't know. The lad's as silent as the grave with me. I should have tried harder, but I know nowt about raising bairns. When William named me guardian, I swore I'd look after his boy—now I've let him and Jenny down." Despite her overwhelming concern for Brand, the bewildered sorrow in Mr. Townsend's voice made Fenella's heart ache.

Her hands clenched in her skirts. She'd lost Henry. Be...*damned* if she'd lose Brandon, too. Since her husband's death, her love for her son was all that had kept her going. Only in the last few months had she seen a glimmer of a fresh start. Her friends Caroline Beaumont and Helena Wade had decided that five years of mourning were enough for any woman and they'd dragged her back into society.

With a determined gesture, she set her untouched brandy next to her embroidery. "Let's go, then."

Mr. Townsend regarded her blankly as she stood. "Go?"

"Yes. I'm coming with you back to Eton."

"That's impossible, my dear Lady Deerham."

"No, it's not. And while we argue, the boys get further out of reach."

The emphatic brows—heaven help her, everything on Mr. Townsend was larger than life—drew together over his eyes. "There's no way I'm taking you. I don't have time to cater to a lady's requirements."

Fenella's lips tightened at his quick dismissal of her usefulness and endurance. For five years, people had coddled her—if truth were told, people had always coddled her—and she'd had enough. It had been unpleasant, but refreshingly bracing when Mr. Townsend had shouted at her. Nobody ever shouted at her. Since her widowhood, they were inclined to murmur in her presence as if they were in church.

"I won't hold you up," she said evenly.

"Of course you will." He leveled a telling look upon her. "I mean…look at you. You'd crack with one careless touch."

Her eyes narrowed. "Looks can deceive, sir. I've borne a child. I've lost a beloved husband. I've made a life for myself." Well, at least, thanks to Helena and

Caro, she was trying to turn that last claim into reality. "Don't patronize me, Mr. Townsend. A moment's weakness does not a weakling make."

"My dear Lady Deerham, you can't go traipsing off into the night with a man you don't know. There will be a scandal."

"Believe me, sir, your reputation is safe." If he called her his dear lady again, she'd go after him with a fire iron. "And even if it's not, I promise you don't have to marry me."

He didn't smile. "You speak lightly, but you haven't considered the consequences. My reputation in society doesn't matter a tinker's damn. Nobody's likely to worry about my suitability for Almack's. You, on the other hand, move in more discriminating circles."

It was a good argument, she gave him that. But not good enough when her beloved son was in danger. "I'm coming with you."

"You can trust me with Brandon, you know."

Surprisingly, some deep instinct insisted that, despite his rough edges, Mr. Townsend was a good man. In his care, Brand would be safe. But for heaven's sake, she was Brand's mother, and only crushing him in her arms and giving him a good scolding would banish her terror. "I know."

If she expected gratitude for her trust, she was disappointed. He folded his arms over his broad chest and regarded her like an insect. "Then let me do this. I'll send word as soon as I find them."

"You won't do that because I'll be right beside you."

"No, you won't. And nothing you say will sway me, madam."

Madam was almost as grating as *my dear Lady Deerham.* "Very well."

He looked relieved. "Excellent. I knew you'd see sense."

She rang for Greaves who appeared so swiftly that he must have been standing outside the door. "Have my gig readied."

"What the devil?" Mr. Townsend snapped. "You said you weren't coming."

"Not with you. I'll follow close on your heels."

"Don't be absurd. You won't keep up."

"I could beat you to Eton with one hand tied behind my back."

Exasperation turned those craggy features forbidding. "Brave words. If I didn't think you'd risk your damned fool neck, I'd take you up on the challenge."

With so much at stake, Fenella couldn't falter. "So you'll take me."

"Not on your life."

"We'll be discreet."

His snort was dismissive. "Aye, and of course nobody will pay a lass like you a scrap of attention when we stop to ask after the scamps."

"We'll manage."

That square jaw jutted with obstinacy. "*I'll* be on my own."

She summoned a saccharine smile, despite her urgency. "And I'll be just behind you."

"You're a blasted stubborn wench, Lady Deerham."

"I am." Strangely the remark pleased her. It was an improvement on madam or his dear Lady Deerham. Somewhere in the last six months, she'd grown a backbone—and she liked it. Before meeting Caroline and Helena, she'd been contemptibly compliant. "Whether you intend to take me or not, I'm leaving for Eton within the next quarter of an hour."

He folded his arms and tilted one eyebrow in disdain. She raised her chin and faced him down, although it was rather like scowling at Ben Nevis and expecting it to melt into a puddle.

"There's no room in my carriage for a maid, my lady. And I've neither time nor inclination to swap my rig for a larger vehicle. We'll be completely alone. You and I. All night."

Fenella recognized the potential for scandal. She hardly cared. "Sir, two young boys are lost somewhere out in the darkness. With or without you, I will find them. Compared to my son's safety, I couldn't give a... tinker's damn for my social standing. Or your nitpicking."

He looked rather startled at her language, despite his own tendency to curse. Too bad. She'd swear like a sailor if it achieved her end of joining him. She wasn't at all sure what she thought of Anthony Townsend. But she was positive of one thing—in the case of trouble,

Mr. Townsend was big and mean enough to handle anything life flung at him. If anyone could track Brand and Carey down, it was this large, belligerent male.

"This is a mistake."

That sounded like he might relent. "The mistake is delaying our departure."

He gestured toward her yellow gown with a contempt her modiste's best efforts didn't deserve. "You'll need to change."

He'd yielded, although he was yet to admit it. She hid a triumphant smile. She faced hours in this mercurial man's company. Silly to get him offside. Or *more* offside. "I'll be quick."

"You'd better be."

The smile at last proved unstoppable, although she hoped it wasn't as smug as it felt. Extraordinary to smile at all. Defying Mr. Townsend bolstered her courage. "You'll take me, then."

His sigh was long-suffering. "Not if you're more than five minutes getting ready—and very much against my better judgment. God help us both."

CHAPTER TWO

$\mathcal{A}$nthony stared helplessly at the ravishing blond sylph in yellow who imagined she could stand up to him. And against all expectations, seemed to have prevailed.

His family was respectable. His father had been a mine manager, so he'd been brought up with a modicum of decency. He'd never gone hungry. He'd had a good education. He'd had an adventurous life, discovering the world and its wonders.

But never in his travels had he seen anything to match Lady Deerham.

Since he'd made his fortune, many a lordling had been eager to take advantage of his business acumen. But ladies remained an unfamiliar breed. Especially ladies like this, as fragile as a new rosebud or the Venetian glass he imported to such great profit. When he'd stopped shouting long enough to notice what she looked like, his mind had immediately turned to custard.

When his brain resumed working, all he knew was how huge and clumsy and unrefined he was compared to her graceful perfection. It was like Caliban yearning after Ariel, if Caliban was a great bear of a blockhead with a booming voice, and hands like dinner plates, and the manners of a stevedore. By rights, she should shrink from his uncouth presence.

But this creature of air and light possessed surprising courage. No common sense at all, of course, or else she'd see that her plans were totally unsuitable.

He definitely knew one thing about gentlewomen. Rules hedged them about, tighter than the strapping on a bale of fine merino wool from New South Wales.

But somehow despite being a foot shorter and half his weight, she'd forced an agreement from him. Another item to add to his list of facts about the nobly born female. They were damned slippery customers.

"Mr. Townsend?"

He must be gawping at her as if she'd clouted him on the noggin with a cricket bat. Which was a fair description of his state. "Aye, you can come. But cause any trouble and I'll unload you at the first inn we come to and send a carriage to collect you when everything's over."

"That's a bargain." Her smile intensified the sensation of having been hit with a blunt instrument.

Dear Lord above, but she was pretty.

She was completely out of his sphere and pointless to want, but nobody could stop a man from taking pleasure in a bonny lass.

When he was alone, he lifted her untouched brandy and downed it in one gulp. Even though he was a fellow of generally abstemious habits.

The liquor hit his throat with a hot burst and shocked him back to the current moment. But as he went outside to check the horses, he could swear he wasn't the same man he'd been half an hour ago.

Anthony had to give Lady Deerham credit. She was downstairs in not much more than the unreasonable five minutes he'd specified. Thank God they delayed. As they descended her front steps toward his curricle, a horseman raced into Curzon Street and flung himself down before them. In the torchlight, he looked filthy and frantic and travel-weary. All the sudden activity made Anthony's highbred horses shift restlessly in their harness, and the footman holding their heads spoke in a low voice to calm them.

"I'm looking for Lady Deerham," the man gasped as another footman ran down to catch the sweating horse. "I've come from Eton College."

Hell, don't let this be more bad news. The rider's manner immediately discounted any chance that the lads were safely back at school. "What is it?" Anthony automatically stepped nearer to Lady Deerham.

"I am Fenella Deerham," she said with admirable dignity. Between the torches and the full moon, Anthony couldn't miss how the blood drained from her porcelain complexion.

"My name's Harley." The man snatched off his hat and bowed quickly, before he fumbled in his coat. "I'm a porter at the school. I've got a letter from the headmaster, my lady."

Anthony was standing close enough to hear her indrawn breath. Without thinking, he took her arm in case she felt faint again. Inside, he'd been astounded how his pulses had leaped at the brief contact. Now he braced for that automatic physical response.

"I'm Anthony Townsend," he said sharply. "Have the lads been located?"

"No, sir." Harley located the letter and extended it toward Lady Deerham.

"But there's news?" Her voice was artificially calm, and Anthony found himself yet again commending her courage.

"We found a letter addressed to you in the outgoing mail. The headmaster took the liberty of opening it. It's enclosed with Dr. Keate's note."

"Thank you." Trembling, Lady Deerham ripped open the letter. Shoving the accompanying papers at Anthony, she feverishly read Brandon's message.

She looked up with appalled eyes. "They've gone to see Carey's old nurse. She's sick."

"At least that explains why they ran away. Mrs. Penn is the closest thing to a mother Carey has left," Anthony said somberly. He turned to Harley. "Surely it would have been better to contact me than trouble her ladyship."

Harley tugged his hat between his hands and looked ill. Anthony Townsend's displeasure generally had that effect, although it hadn't subdued valiant Lady Deerham. "Begging your pardon, Mr. Townsend, but Dr. Keate said you'd most likely be here. If not, I had instructions to ride to your offices once I'd seen her ladyship." He stopped torturing his hat and fished another letter from his coat. "This is for you."

"Has the school sent someone after the boys?" Lady Deerham asked.

"They don't know where they've gone," Harley said.

Anthony took the letter addressed to him. A quick glance confirmed that it contained the same information, if less carefully phrased. "They don't know, but I do."

"Where?" Lady Deerham turned a wide, troubled gaze on him.

"I've recently purchased an estate outside Winchester. I settled some of my brother's staff there, including Mrs. Penn."

Relief flooded the blue eyes. "So we know where to find them."

"If they make it that far."

"Brandon's clever."

"Not clever enough to stay put, damn it. Both of them are completely pudding brained. If Carey had an ounce of good sense, he'd have told me what was going on. He must know I'd take him down to see Penny in a flash."

"Perhaps he didn't know you were due back in England." She passed him her son's letter. "Brand went with Carey because he couldn't let his friend make such a journey alone."

In the back and forth of trying to keep Lady Deerham safely at home, his rage and worry had retreated. Now, seeing her distress, he returned to wanting to shut both boys away on short rations until Christmas. "You sound like you approve," he said sharply.

"I don't. I want to box his ears for putting me through all this. But he's acted from a good heart."

"A good heart and a thick head," Anthony snapped, seeing no excuse for the boys' lack of consideration.

"That's not fair."

"What's not fair is a bairn coddled to the point where he imagines he can do something unforgivable like this and face no consequences."

She'd been pale with fear. Now twin flags of color marked her slanted cheekbones.

"It is you, sir, who is unforgivable." Her voice was sharp and precise enough to etch glass.

He regretted his bluntness the moment he spoke, although he stood by his opinion. Only child of a clinging, overindulgent widow? Stood to reason that the lad was spoiled. Perhaps it was a good thing he and Lady Deerham were likely to remain strangers. "No matter. I'll send your son back to you, shall I? Instead of letting him face the punishment he deserves at school?"

However hackneyed the image, he'd thought of her eyes as limpid pools. Now they flashed blue lightning, and any idea of limpid vanished forever.

"You won't send my son anywhere, Mr. Townsend. I'll come with you to collect him, and make my own arrangements to bring him home."

Not this again. Silly wench didn't know when she was beaten. "Now we know where they're headed, there's no reason for you to join me. I give you my word I'll find the lads."

The audible scoff was incongruous coming from such a refined creature. "As if I'd trust you with my son, Mr. Townsend. You're likely to *coddle* him into a beating."

When he'd learned her Christian name, just now, he'd thought it suited her. Now he wasn't so sure. A Fenella should be amiable and obedient, not a raging virago. Better she'd been called Boadicea.

At the top of the steps, the butler cleared his throat. "My lady, shall I take Mr. Harley into the kitchens for some refreshment after his long ride? And there's no need for the footmen to stand in the cold if you and the gentleman wish to continue chatting."

Anthony had lost all awareness of his surroundings, including the audience for his quarrel. An avidly listening, curious audience as one quick glance at Harley indicated.

This time, Lady Deerham flushed with chagrin. Never in his life had he met a female with such an expressive face. A quality he regretted now she glared at him with bitter dislike. She turned to Greaves. "Yes, of course take Mr. Harley. And please bring the gig around."

Anthony barely bit back a growl, but he had the sense to soften his voice. "Don't be a little fool. You don't know where my estate is."

"Outside Winchester, I believe you mentioned," she said with a poisonous sweetness that lifted the hairs on the back of his neck. "I'm sure even a little fool can manage to find her way from there."

She was right, blast her. The prospect of her trailing him all the way to the Beeches was insupportable. For the first time when he surveyed her, his impulse wasn't a mad urge to fall to his knees and worship her extraordinary beauty. Instead he fought the overpowering need to give her a good shake, until she conceded he was in charge of the rescue mission. She should jolly well obey his instructions, and stay fiddling with her embroidery in her pretty jewel box of a townhouse, while he rode off to slay dragons.

He retained just enough self-awareness to recognize the essential absurdity of that thought. But only just.

So instead of flinging this troublesome female over his shoulder and marching inside to lock her in the attics, he did something almost as shocking.

"Oh, for pity's sake," he snarled, catching her firmly by the willowy waist and tossing her up into his curricle.

"Mr. Townsend!"

"Be quiet and hold on," he said curtly, rounding the carriage and leaping into the driving seat.

"Good luck, my lady," the butler said, stepping forward and sliding a valise into the back of the curricle. Right now Anthony might want to strangle Lady Deerham, but he had a suspicion he could come to like her butler.

"You're kidnapping me," she said under her breath as Anthony grabbed the reins. His two fine chestnuts shook their harness until it jingled. They were as impatient to be on their way as he was.

"You wanted to come," he grunted. "Now time is of the essence. We know the lads' destination, but they've got miles to cover first."

She directed a doubtful frown at his grip on the reins. That pricked at his vanity. She clearly fancied herself as a whip, although he couldn't imagine this ethereal creature controlling much beyond a sleepy pony.

She's controlled you, hasn't she?

He ignored the snide voice in his mind and shouted to the footman holding his horses' heads. "Let them go."

"Godspeed, my lady," the butler called as Anthony clattered off at a punishing rate, two runaways to find, and a sulky fairy princess fuming by his side.

CHAPTER THREE

As they sped through the freezing night toward Hampshire, Fenella was almost glad that Mr. Townsend gave her such good cause to dislike him. It helped to distract her from picturing what might happen to Brand and Carey. Every time she thought of her son alone and unprotected—and she couldn't think of much else—her stomach cramped with nausea.

Dear God, let Brand be safe.

At this hour, the roads were mostly empty, although farmers would soon be on their way into London with their produce. Winter hadn't yet stuck its claws into the year, but the wind whistling around her ears as they plunged through the night promised frosts ahead. With every shiver, she prayed that the boys were somewhere safe and warm.

Fenella wasn't by nature a sullen woman. Pique didn't come easily. With every mile they covered, the distance between her and her monumental companion became increasingly awkward.

Not, alas, the physical distance.

Mr. Townsend was such a…substantial figure that the cramped seat crushed her up against him, closer than she'd been to any man since Henry's death. Inevitably, as their bodies rubbed together in the jolting carriage, his radiating heat and the clean, salty scent of his skin became part of her landscape. She could believe that he'd docked today. He smelled like the sea.

He didn't smell like a villain and a bully. He smelled like a healthy male in his prime, and much as she fought it, that evocative scent reminded Fenella how she'd missed a man's physical presence over the last lonely years. After Henry's death, she'd missed his cheerfulness and unwavering devotion. She'd missed sharing her joys and sorrows with him. She'd missed his love.

But her proximity to Mr. Townsend was an uncomfortable reminder that she'd missed Henry's body, too. Not just the act of love—although she'd woken from countless sensual dreams to the aching realization that Henry Deerham lay in the grave's eternal embrace—but the pleasures of having a man about the place. Masterful, direct Anthony Townsend couldn't be more different from laughing, goodhearted Henry Deerham, but despite her antipathy, tonight's journey stirred senses long dormant.

She mightn't like Mr. Townsend. In fact, she was convinced she didn't. But plastered to his side, she was inescapably aware of his overpowering masculinity. And that made her ashamed. She'd been a good and faithful wife to Henry. Thinking of another man in... those terms made her feel like she broke his trust.

True to his word, when Mr. Townsend stopped to change horses, he waited only long enough for the ostlers to hitch up the new team before he set off once again. Fenella felt him silently daring her to complain, but she made no request for a delay. He misunderstood her if he imagined she meant to impede this desperate hunt.

More biting cold and breathtaking speed, and gradually her reasonable side gained the upper hand. Resentment became less satisfying by the minute. While Mr. Townsend's comment had been unfortunate, he'd been half out of his mind with worry about Carey. And perhaps there was a shred of truth in what he'd said, much as she loathed admitting it. Since Henry's death, she and Brand had depended so closely on each other.

She was on the verge of saying something inane about the weather, if only to ease the bristling atmosphere, when Mr. Townsend spoke for what felt like the first time in hours. "We're lucky with the full moon."

"Yes."

For the life of her, she couldn't think of anything to

add. She fidgeted with the rug he'd pushed at her when they started out. His care for her comfort had surprised her when he'd been so set on leaving her behind.

As they covered another mile without speaking, she sensed his disappointment at her lack of response. So far, she'd avoided looking at him. Not because she was angry—by now, she was over her huff—but because staring at him intensified that unacceptable female awareness. Now she couldn't help snatching a quick glimpse at his set, angular features. He looked hard and purposeful, as she'd come to expect, but also discouraged.

Hours of travel on an icy night stretched ahead. She should say something, if only to break this prickly silence. They had the boys in common, but she flinched from inviting more criticism.

She was at the point of asking how far they had to go to his estate when he spoke again. "I'm sorry, Lady Deerham. I have no right to judge the way you raise your son. It's none of my business."

To her surprise, instead of graciously accepting the apology, she found herself explaining. "You weren't entirely wrong. I did coddle Brandon after Henry died at Waterloo. I couldn't help it."

"You must have loved your husband very much."

"I do. I always will." She stared sightlessly over the horses' ears to the road winding between the fields. Thick hedges rose on either side, creating an illusion of intimacy. "I hope—I know—since then I've always acted in my son's best interests, despite my instincts to keep him close and safe beside me. You have no idea how difficult it was to send Brand to school, but he needed some masculine influence."

"Now the school hasn't proven the safe haven you'd hoped."

"No."

"Tragedy can strike anywhere," he said softly. "Look at William and Jenny. A storm out of nowhere on the loveliest day in summer."

Fenella gripped her gloved hands together in her lap. She was physically weary, but too keyed up to sleep. Her mind was in such turmoil, she felt as alert and on edge as a mouse in a cat club. Strangely, despite their short but rocky relationship, talking to Mr. Townsend kept her from falling victim to phantom horrors. Something about him inspired confidence. His strength and solidity perhaps. More likely his self-assurance.

"Were you close to your brother?"

"Aye."

Again, Fenella recognized the sorrow beneath the clipped response. "Perhaps that's why Carey and Brandon so swiftly became friends—they both lost people they love."

Mr. Townsend sighed. "Brandon has you. Poor Carey drew the short straw when he was left in my care."

His bitterness surprised her. "You don't mean that."

His lips twisted in self-derision. "Don't I?"

"You obviously love the boy. When you burst into my house, you were beside yourself with fear. And as your ward, he'll never want for anything."

"Anything material, at least. If they're to thrive, children need more than food in their bellies and somewhere to sleep."

"But he must know you love him. I picked it up immediately, even through the bluster."

"Perhaps I should bluster at him more often so he understands," Mr. Townsend said dourly.

She bit back her impatient response that if his guardian just told Carey that he loved him, the problem would disappear. Living with a husband and a son had taught her that males preferred to sidestep direct declarations of feeling, however useful they might be.

"Then you just have to try harder to show him that you love him," she said calmly. "For a start, you could spend more time together."

Surprised dark eyes left the road to focus on her. "You don't mince your words."

She shrugged. "You're the adult. It's up to you to find some way through this."

He gave a grunt of amusement. "For a woman who looks likely to snap in a gentle breeze, you punch above your weight, Lady Deerham."

His compliment, backhanded as it was, pleased her.

All her life, people—men—had told her she was pretty. Very few had remarked on her strength.

This time when they changed horses, Mr. Townsend stepped down from the carriage and came around to offer her a hand. "We'll have something to eat."

"I'd rather keep going."

Was that admiration glinting in his eyes? Her heart kicked, before she reminded herself she had more important things to worry about than Mr. Townsend's opinion of her. "Ten minutes for a hot drink and some bread and cheese won't hurt."

"Ten? I thought the limit was five."

His face remained perfectly straight as he assisted her to alight into a yard bustling with men and horses. "I'm feeling generous."

Fenella dipped her head as she entered the crowded hostelry on Mr. Townsend's arm. Someone making a late return from the Ascot races might recognize her. But nobody paid any attention to the well-dressed couple. As they stepped inside, Mr. Townsend murmured to the landlord, and she found herself in a private parlor, small and cozy with a roaring fire.

"I'll check the horses. Sit down and warm up. I won't be long."

"Thank you," she said, crossing the room to stand before the fire. She sucked in a breath, relieved that she was no longer crushed up against Mr. Townsend. She couldn't blame him for that insidious proximity. She'd insisted on coming. But it was much easier to remember she was a widow with a child and not a giddy girl when he stood safely on the other side of the room.

She stripped off her gloves and extended bare hands toward the flames. The heat set the blood in her chilled fingers tingling.

When the door opened behind her, she didn't look around.

Until a man who wasn't Mr. Townsend addressed her in the slurred tones of the deeply inebriated.

As Anthony turned into the short corridor leading to the parlor, some drunken ass ahead of him let out a triumphant bray of laughter. Alarm tightened his gut. Hell, he'd only been away a few minutes.

He lengthened his stride and careered round the corner to hear some tipsy, extravagantly dressed coxcomb announce, "Well, what do we have here? A pretty yella-haired strumpet looking for company. I've had the devil's luck today, boys."

The well-bred imbecile stood between two equally gormless companions who craned past him to see into the room where Anthony had left Lady Deerham.

Everything inside Anthony's head turned red. He barged up to the trio and shoved them out of the way.

How dare anyone accost Fenella? Couldn't they see that she was his?

That thought jolted him into pausing before he started flinging his fists around and creating bloody mayhem.

"I'll say this once, then the trouble's on you," he grated out, battling the impulse to thump the idiots into oblivion anyway. "Go back to the taproom now."

One glance at Anthony and the two offsiders edged away on unsteady legs. "Your pardon, sir. A mistake. No offense meant," one bleated.

Their vocal friend swayed on the spot. Too far gone in his cups to see the danger, he leveled a bleary gaze at Anthony. "Demme, you're a dashed big 'un."

He was young. All three were. Barely twenty, if he reckoned aright. But after sailing the world, Anthony was regrettably familiar with the trouble even very young men could cause. His aggressive stance didn't relax. "I won't ask again."

The young man raised a shaky quizzing glass to his eye, then, recklessly, directed his inspection into the room. His lustful smile told its own story. "The doxy's a prime article. I'll give you a thousand guineas for her."

Before Anthony could pulverize the upstart, clear laughter rang out from inside the room. "My husband may just take you up on that, sir. But in the meantime, why don't you go and sleep it off?"

Astonishment kept Anthony's fists by his sides. Fenella's courage should no longer catch him unawares, but still she took his breath away. The lout was right—she *was* a prime article.

At the sound of Lady Deerham's unmistakably upper-class voice, the youth flushed blotchy red and backed away from the door. He cast a quick glance at Anthony and this time, he took in how much muscle threatened to obliterate him. "Your pardon. I saw the ladybird…uh, the lady on her own, and I thought—"

"I know what you thought," Anthony said wearily. "Leave the ladies be, at least until you can see straight."

The lad bowed and retreated after his friends with much haste and no dignity.

Anthony sighed and entered the room. "Husband?"

To his surprise, the heroine of the hour blushed. "It was the best I could think of at the time."

"I'm sorry about that. I shouldn't have left you."

Even more surprising, her smile glowed with open approval. "You came to my rescue."

His heart performed a strange skipping dance, and his mind went flying out of the room. He blinked at her and told himself that he was too old to fall victim to a pretty wench's smile.

And didn't believe a word of it.

To hide his confusion, he turned to close the door. "You were perfectly capable of handling that silly bit of wet string."

"Perhaps." She sat at the small table with a grace that set his wayward heart capering again. What in God's name was wrong with him? "It turned out I didn't have to. Thank you."

He sat opposite her. "On second thought, a thousand guineas is a lot of money."

"Perhaps you should check if the offer's still open," she said tranquilly. "It would save you hauling me all the way to Hampshire."

She was magnificent—and not just because she was the loveliest woman he'd ever seen. He had no doubt that she was still deathly afraid for her son. And having strange men accost them in a public house would give most ladies the vapors. But she glided through it all with perfect composure.

In London, he'd resigned himself to putting up with a delicate female who found rough travel insupportable. But she'd been as game as a terrier the whole way and hadn't complained once. Even when that inebriated oaf had marched in on her.

A thousand guineas? Ten thousand wouldn't do her justice.

Either he needed to revisit his opinion of upperclass women as basically useless. Or Fenella Deerham was a glorious exception to the rule.

"Actually you haven't been much trouble," he said gruffly. "I might let the lad keep his winnings, instead of spending them on wild women like you."

She was still smiling and his heart returned to cavorting in a most disconcerting manner. "My hero."

The arrival of two mugs of steaming beef tea and a

meat pie saved Anthony from responding to her dry remark. But some previously unknown corner of his soul turned romantic and yearned to believe that she meant it.

Which was the most worrying thing of all.

CHAPTER FOUR

Fenella and Mr. Townsend set off from the inn not long afterward, and despite her qualms about the delay, she felt better for the short break and the meal. Even with the added entertainment.

That encounter between Mr. Townsend and the drunken stripling had been telling. It confirmed her suspicion that his earlier behavior wasn't typical. More than her safety—after all, she could have screamed for help if necessary—she'd been afraid her escort might start a brawl which would lead to unbearable delays. But Mr. Townsend had handled the boy with aplomb, and saved both Fenella and their quest. Those huge fists could have made his point, but he'd used his brain instead.

He became more interesting by the hour.

She tucked her chin into the rug to escape the

strengthening wind. One gloved hand clutched the side of the rig against the swaying.

"Why don't you try and sleep?" he murmured as they sped past the high walls of some sleeping estate. Since leaving the inn, they'd spoken only a word or two, but the antagonism had vanished.

"I can't." Every time she closed her eyes, she saw Brand coming to grief. Hurt and lying in a ditch. Lost in a wood. Worst of all, struggling to escape some faceless villain's clutches.

"Worrying won't find the lads any quicker."

"I know," she said regretfully. "If it did, they'd be home right now."

"We're still a couple of hours from the Beeches."

She tugged the rug up higher, although cuddled up against Mr. Townsend, she wasn't cold. "I'm perfectly fine."

"You're as taut as a sail in a high wind," he said.

She blushed to realize that their physical nearness left her few secrets. But what did that matter when her son was lost? Her hand clenched on the side of the carriage, and she stared out across the moonlit landscape. All she could hear was the horses' hooves, the creak of the curricle, and the whistling wind. They combined into an ominous chant.

You're too late. You're too late.

"Stop expecting the worst," Mr. Townsend said, without taking his attention from the road.

"I can't help it," she muttered. "Perhaps...perhaps if you talk to me, it will help."

"Talk?" He sounded like she'd asked him to turn somersaults in midair.

"Yes. Please. Something to take my mind off the boys."

"I live to serve."

"I doubt it."

"What shall we discuss, my lady? The latest fashion in bonnets? Prinny's plans for the coronation? The best recipe for syllabub?"

"No," she said, appreciating his efforts to ease her distress. She'd misjudged Mr. Townsend on their first meeting. He was far from a boor and a bully. "I'd like to know about you."

"Me." The flat tone conveyed no enthusiasm.

"Yes. Tell me about your life."

"There isn't much to say."

"I don't believe that."

"Well, not much to interest a lady like you."

"You needn't give me all the grisly details." She was positive there had been grisly details. He was too capable not to have encountered and overcome trouble in his life. "I don't know... For example, were you born with money?"

"No. Can't you tell from the way I speak?"

"I...I like the way you speak. It's real."

Many men dragged themselves up in the world. Most aped the aristocracy, usually not very well. She admired the way Mr. Townsend didn't try to hide where he came from. Despite his humble origins, he was a proud man—and given his success, he had every right to his pride.

A grunt of sardonic amusement. "It is, at that."

"Well?"

He sighed. "Wouldn't you rather tell me about yourself?"

"No. That means talking about Brand. And right now—"

He spoke before she finished. That was something else she liked about Mr. Townsend. He was quick on the uptake. "My father was a mine manager in South Yorkshire. An honest, hardworking man. My mother was a foreigner."

"A foreigner?" she asked, intrigued.

His firm mouth relaxed a fraction. "Aye, from Lancashire."

She gave a short laugh. "How exotic."

"There were four of us children. William was ten years older than me. I have two sisters, both married with half a dozen bairns between them. I'm the youngest."

"Spoiled, no doubt?"

Then she was sorry she asked because it might remind him of their quarrel. But he continued in that easy bass baritone. "Aye. A right little terror. Local opinion had it that I'd end up hanged at the crossroads before I was done. But I turned into a solid enough citizen in the end. Once I finished my schooling at sixteen, I joined William in the shipping line he'd set up in Liverpool, mainly trading to America. That's when William Townsend Shipping became Townsend and Co."

"And you worked your magic from the start?" The rumbling voice with its northern burr settled her jumping nerves in a most miraculous way. She was still afraid for Brand, but at least Mr. Townsend's life story helped her concentrate on something other than possible calamities.

"No. The vile tyrant made me work my way up through the business." Affection deepened his voice when he spoke of his brother. "I started as a clerk. At a clerk's wages."

"Oh, foul injustice. I'm sure you didn't like that."

"Not at first. But I quickly learned that numbers are key in business. Luckily all that schooling had made me a wizard with arithmetic."

She sighed in mock disappointment. "I'd imagined wild foreign adventures. Pirates. Mutinies. Treasure hunts. Lovely dusky maidens. Exploring unknown lands."

"You're a romantic, lass."

He'd called her lass a couple of times. Something silly and feminine in her melted into syrup every time he did. "Perhaps. Or perhaps your heroics at the inn turned my head."

"Aye. I'm a right knight in shining armor."

"So you did the books, and honed your financial genius, and eventually took over the company?"

"No. After a year or so, William took pity on me and put me to work on the ships as a common sailor."

"At a common sailor's wages?"

"You're a right sharp lass," he said. "Aye. But I didn't mind. I was out of England and discovering life. It was an exciting time for a lad of eighteen. By that stage, I'd convinced him to venture further afield than Massachusetts."

"I knew you'd had adventures," she said, pleased. "How I envy your travels. I've never been anywhere, when you've seen the whole world."

"Most of it. China and Brazil and New South Wales and India and Russia, at the very least."

"Will you tell me about them?" she asked.

So he did. And the carriage ate up the miles without her noticing, as he entertained her with tales of incredible deeds in far-flung places like Siam and the Indies and the South Pacific.

Fenella stirred from vividly colored dreams of foreign lands. All featuring a larger-than-life, dark-haired man who took every danger in his stride. It was easy to dream of danger when she felt so deliciously warm and safe.

Then she remembered Brandon, and she made a sound of distress.

"Hush, lass," an impossibly deep voice purred just beneath her ear.

Oh, dear. She was curled up against Mr. Townsend, her head resting on his shoulder. He'd wrapped his greatcoat around both of them so she felt marvelously cocooned and cherished.

And she realized with an unpleasant shock quite how far she'd come from the woman who'd set out in his company, convinced he was an unmannerly brute.

Flustered she began to fight against the restricting coat. "Let me up."

"Give me a second," he said gently and swiftly unwound her.

Clumsily she lurched to sit up. Her eyes were scratchy with tiredness, and she rolled her head to ease stiff neck muscles. Bare, wintry farmland stretched around them. The moon sat low on the horizon.

"I went to sleep." The words emerged as an accusation.

"Only for half an hour. I warned you that my life was a dull topic."

She'd been anything but bored with his adventures in all those fairytale places. But that hypnotic voice, the long journey, and the quiet night had caught up with her.

"I'm sorry. I was lying all over you. How very... embarrassing. And how on earth could I sleep with

Brandon in danger?" Self-disgust weighted her voice. Her ease with Mr. Townsend betrayed not only Brand, but Henry as well.

"You'd fretted yourself into exhaustion. It's a cold night, and I'm large and warm."

"Still, it's not…"

He saved her from struggling for words to express her confused feelings. "We're nearly at the Beeches," he said calmly.

She tugged the rug up around her hot cheeks, and told herself she was just tired and worried and overemotional. "Surely if the boys came this way, we'd have caught sight of them by now."

"Who knows how long they were gone before the school discovered they were missing?" He turned the carriage between an impressive pair of gateposts crowned with stone lions. "If they found transport, they could beat us by hours."

"Or they could have met with harm."

His glance was reproving. "Don't lose your nerve now. You've been a pillar of strength so far. If they're not at the house, all isn't lost. We'll retrace our journey and track them down."

As they bowled along a beech-lined drive, Fenella fought the urge to clutch at Mr. Townsend's brawny arm like a child seeking reassurance. "You sound very certain."

"Carey is a clever lad. I don't know much about him,

but I know that. And his friend is blessed with courage and resourcefulness."

Startled, she stared at him. "How can you know that?"

For the first time, Mr. Townsend smiled fully. And despite fretting over Brandon, Fenella felt her world shift on its axis.

When she'd first seen Anthony Townsend, she'd considered him striking rather than attractive. Stern. Commanding. Monumental. But his smile made him look younger and more approachable. She realized with a shock that he couldn't be much older than her own thirty. No more than thirty-five, certainly. The lopsided curve of his lips over his large white teeth, and the humor lighting those dark brown eyes turned him into a man of more than ordinary appeal.

Smiling, he was breathtakingly charming. And dazzlingly attractive.

Dear heaven, she was in trouble.

"Because his mother is an exceptional woman."

Since her recent emergence from mourning, she'd laughed away a thousand extravagant compliments. None made her blush like Mr. Townsend's unexpected praise. She wasn't sure what to say, but luckily a huge stone pile of a building came into view and saved her.

"Goodness me," she gasped in awe.

He laughed softly. "If I'm playing the country gentleman, I'm going to do it right."

"No half measures?"

"None at all."

"Aren't we going to see Carey's old nurse?" After the troubling revelation that somewhere between London and the Beeches, she'd developed an unwelcome penchant for this complex man, she was grateful to retreat to prosaic matters.

Following her one true love's death, she'd sworn to devote herself to her duty as a mother. It hadn't felt like a sacrifice. She'd loved once. She never wanted to love again. Anyway, the prospect of ever finding another man attractive had been so remote as to seem impossible.

For nearly five years, she'd locked herself away with memories of her young husband and their life together. Even re-entering society this year hadn't pierced her essential isolation.

But now, she wondered if she was over life after all. Tonight long-buried feelings stirred, and she resented it. She had no wish to brave the hurly-burly of attraction. Losing love had nearly destroyed her. She couldn't risk going through that again.

"Nanny Penn lives in the east wing." He drew the horses to a stop on the circular drive before the sprawling stone house with its rows of tall windows and imposing columned portico.

"Lucky Nanny Penn," she said faintly.

"I bought it after I came to a house party. I haven't decided what I'll do with it. I still haven't been over the whole house—or the grounds."

"You bought it. Without seeing all of it?"

"Aye," he said, as if that was nothing extraordinary.

Fenella had never known want, and she moved in the highest social circles. But the thought of having the cash to pick up an entire estate on a whim made her finally accept the gossip about Mr. Townsend's wealth.

He leaped down with a vigor that belied his night of driving, and moved to offer his hand. She shivered as she accepted his help, not entirely because he'd taken his big, warm body away. "It might have had a leaky roof or dry rot. The fields might be prone to flooding."

"I sent a team of surveyors and farming experts down before I signed anything. I'm not one of your careless aristocrats, my lady. I work hard for my brass, and my brass works hard for me."

"So the building is sound?"

"It's rundown. That's how I persuaded old Grantley to sell. He didn't have the cash for repairs. Now I plan to turn this into a place Carey will be proud to come home to."

She couldn't fault his concern for his nephew. And knowing how he cared, she found the courage to catch his arm as he turned away to check the horses. At her touch, he went stock still. Whereas her words faded to nothing under the heat sizzling through her at the contact.

She snatched her hand away and stared bewildered at him. She was acting like a silly schoolgirl. And it wasn't as if they'd never touched before. In her opinion, there had been far too much touching since Mr. Townsend had blown into her drawing room like a tropical hurricane.

She swallowed to ease the inexplicable tightness in her throat. "You'll think I'm presumptuous."

His mouth quirked. "I'm a plain man who appreciates plain speaking. Surely you've worked that out, Lady Deerham."

"In that case, I hope you'll listen to a little well-meant advice."

"Go ahead," he said neutrally as a groom ran out from the side of the house to take charge of the horses.

She lowered her voice. "I know you're angry with Carey, and you think he ought to be punished."

Mr. Townsend folded his arms and regarded her with an unreadable expression. How she wished the light was better so she could interpret his reaction to her interference. "He's caused needless inconvenience and upset. I'm hoping that's all he's caused, and there are no other unfortunate consequences from this prank."

"Yes, he has. But you love the boy and want to build his trust."

"You're asking me to tiptoe around what he's done?"

"I'm asking you not to go in with all guns blazing."

"The way I did with you?"

What was the point of lying? "Yes."

"So I just pat him on the head and say no harm done?"

She sighed. "If they're both safe—and I pray they are —no harm *has* been done." When he didn't answer, she plowed on. "Just give him a chance to explain before you start tearing strips off him."

"What a poor opinion you have of me."

"Not at all. Not...now." She stopped before she said too much. Anyway, this was about Carey, not her mixed-up responses to Mr. Townsend. "Because your emotions are engaged, it would be so easy to make a fatal misstep and create a gulf between you. I want what's best for Carey. And...for you."

During a tense interval, he stared into her face as though he probed her soul. Then he nodded briefly. "I promise I'll listen to him. Beyond that, we'll see."

That was the best she'd achieve, she could see. She must be satisfied with his promise and pray that his temper didn't win out.

In most things, he was a reasonable man. But there was such guilt and anger, sorrow and love wrapped up in his feelings for his nephew that she wasn't sure which way he'd jump when he saw Carey.

"Thank you," she said quietly, and let him take her arm as they mounted the wide steps to the imposing front door.

CHAPTER FIVE

he winter dawn was a pale glow on the horizon when Anthony strode up to the door and brought the heavy lion-headed knocker down with a crash. At his side, bonny, brave Fenella Deerham stood silent, but he felt her willing him to tread carefully. Odd how she could do that. He'd never in his life been so aware of another person's thoughts. If anyone asked him, he'd wager he could repeat every word that she *wasn't* saying right now.

By the time the bolt scraped back, he was half frozen and stamping his feet to restore circulation. In the growing light, Fenella looked pale with cold and worry. He wished propriety permitted him to put his arm around her—purely for warmth, of course.

But one did not hug a lady without invitation. Even if she'd been snuggled up against him all night, soft and fragrant and alluringly female.

The door squeaked open to reveal an old man. "Mr. Townsend. We were expecting you."

The butler's words roused tentative hope. "Good morning, Probert. Are the lads here?"

"Yes, sir. They arrived last night."

Anthony drew what felt like his first full breath since he'd discovered Carey missing from Eton. Joy bubbled up inside him like a fountain until he wanted to fling his arms around Fenella and dance into the house.

"Are they well?" she asked, to Anthony's regret withdrawing her hand. Having her on his arm gave him the same sense of rightness he'd felt when he first saw the Beeches.

"Yes, madam. They arrived tired and hungry, but nothing a good meal and some sleep won't fix."

"Oh, thank God," she whispered, sagging with relief. Tears glittered in her fine blue eyes. Anthony caught her elbow, as much an excuse to touch her as to stop her falling.

"Probert, this is Lady Deerham."

She stiffened her backbone and gathered her composure. "Good morning, Probert."

The butler bowed, giving no indication that an unchaperoned tonnish lady bowling up to the house at daybreak was unusual. When they all knew how improper it was.

Probert stepped back to allow them into the hall. Black and white tiles covered the floor. A glass dome crowned the lofty space. A curving double staircase rose to unite into one a story above. The space was breathtakingly impressive, but that didn't explain why it made Anthony's heart sing. He was a plain working man, but from the first, the Beeches had been home.

Anthony struggled to think through the storm of relief. "Please send a groom to the school to let them know that the boys are here."

"We sent a message when they arrived, sir."

"Thank you." He turned to Fenella. "Shall we roust them from their beds?"

To his surprise, she shook her head. "No, they need to rest after their adventures. I can wait, now I know they're safe."

The more he saw of her, the more he liked her. "Shall we look in on Brandon? We'll make sure we don't disturb him."

Her grateful smile proved unsettling for Anthony's heart rate. "Oh, I would like that."

"Where did you put them, Probert?"

"In the blue and green bedrooms, sir."

"Excellent."

"I'll wake cook and have her start breakfast."

"Thank you. We've been traveling all night. Sustenance will be welcome."

"How is Carey's nurse?" Fenella asked.

"Still poorly, I'm sorry to say, but she rallied when she saw the boys. She told young Master Carey off very sharply for running away from school. After that, she looked better than she had all week."

Anthony laughed appreciatively. "Good for her."

"Mr. Townsend, I may be speaking out of turn, but it was clear Master Carey's motives were good, however ill-advised his actions."

Anthony cast Fenella a wry glance as he gestured her toward the graceful staircase. "So I understand, Probert. If someone could sort out some coffee in the next few minutes, they'll have my eternal gratitude."

"Immediately, sir. And I'll set the fire in the morning room."

As they climbed the stairs, Fenella was fine-drawn with tension. He knew her mind wouldn't rest until she'd seen her son with her own two eyes.

Anthony carefully opened the door to the green bedroom, grateful it didn't creak like the front door. The curtains were closed, but he made out a heap of blankets and a tuft of fair hair. This must be Brandon. Carey was as swarthy as his uncle.

Fenella released a shuddering breath as she ventured a couple of steps inside, before retreating on soundless feet. She lingered in the doorway, her face luminous with love, and Anthony had to look away. It was like looking into her soul, and the experience was too heady for someone little more than a stranger.

Reluctance weighted her movements as she shut the door on her sleeping son. Anthony touched her arm in silent comfort, propriety be damned. Swift heat slammed him. Because inevitably, he wanted her. Even shouting at her, he'd wanted her.

He spent his life dealing in the world's finest goods. Silks. Porcelain. Glassware. Expensive trinkets to arouse the appetites of jaded rich men—and women. He'd early learned to appreciate quality.

Fenella Deerham was quality from head to toe.

"Wake him up and talk to him," he whispered. "I know you want to."

Her smile was wistful, and to his surprise she didn't break the contact. "Of course I want to. But he'll be exhausted."

Beautiful and unselfish. She really was a jewel.

And a lady, he reminded himself. Counted among the bluest bloods in the land. While Anthony Townsend's blood was as common as mud.

The world might say he looked too high in setting his sights on Sir Henry Deerham's widow. He wasn't so humble as to agree.

Thoughtfully he opened the next door along the corridor. Carey was a more restless sleeper than his friend. He'd kicked the blankets to the floor, and he lay slantwise across the mattress, his white nightshirt tangled around his wiry body.

Grief pierced Anthony. William had been just such a wriggler. "He's so like his father."

Sympathy softened Fenella's expression. "Those echoes of a lost loved one are painful—and wonderful, aren't they?"

"You understand."

"Of course I do."

"Is Brandon like his father?"

"No, more like me, but occasional moments—expressions or gestures—turn him into Henry's spitting image."

When she mentioned her late husband, her voice held a special note. Anthony couldn't doubt that she'd loved the man she'd married. Nor had he missed the way she'd referred to her love for Henry Deerham in the present tense.

He was ashamed to admit that he wasn't nearly as unselfish as she was. Unworthy jealousy soured his gut.

Their whispered conversation had lasted too long. The long, lean boy in the bed, all arms and legs, stirred and made a sleepy sound of inquiry. "Uncle Tony?"

"Sorry to wake you, old son," he said. "Go back to sleep. It's still early."

Instead of obeying, Carey pushed himself up against the pillows and regarded Anthony warily from under a thick shock of black hair. "You're livid, aren't you?"

Fenella's eyes focused on Anthony in a silent plea for mercy. In truth, his anger had faded. With both lads safe, this adventure concluded happily.

And Carey's antics had cast Fenella Deerham in his path.

Which didn't mean his nephew would evade a stern lecture about responsibility. But not at the crack of dawn. And not when the dark eyes watching him so charily were such a reminder of William.

"I'm not pleased," he said drily. "But a month on bread and water will be punishment enough."

"Bread and..." The boy's thin face broke into an uneasy smile. "You're joking."

"Maybe," Anthony said. "You'll find out at breakfast."

"You're a good sport, Uncle Tony. Papa always said so."

"Well, let's hope your father was right."

The lad yawned widely. "Papa was always right."

"You've given quite a few people a fright. Not least me. I was worried that you ran away because you hated having me as your guardian." It was a difficult admission to make, but the thought had tormented him from the first.

Carey shot him a direct look. "Of course I don't hate you being my guardian. I hate...I hate that my parents aren't here, but I like you, Uncle Tony. And you've been devilish kind to me."

He had to clear a lump of emotion from his throat before he spoke. "I hate that your parents aren't here, too."

"Because you have to look after me?"

Apparently he wasn't alone in needing reassurance. "No, because I miss them."

"I do, too." Now he wasn't awaiting the wrath of God—or at least his uncle—Carey turned his drowsy attention to Fenella. "Cor, Brand didn't exaggerate about his mother being a looker. The miniature doesn't do her justice."

She laughed. "Why, thank you," she said unsteadily. "I think."

"Mind your manners—and your language, young man. You're still on thin ice, remember?"

"Yes, Uncle Tony," Carey said in a subdued voice, but mischief glittered in his eyes. "Good night."

"Good morning," he corrected. "And we'll see you later."

As Anthony pulled the door shut behind them, there was a drowsy murmur from the bed. "Thank you, Uncle Tony. I knew you'd turn up sweet when we came to the sharp end."

"Brat," he said, and Carey chuckled sleepily in response.

"You said he was afraid of you," Fenella said as they started down the corridor.

"I thought he was," Anthony said in a wondering voice. "I've got not much more than a peep out of him since his parents died."

"Perhaps you weren't at ease with him either. And you both had to deal with a terrible tragedy."

"I didn't know what to do with myself, let alone how to comfort a grieving child." He cleared his throat. "Carey should have been on the yacht, too, but he broke his arm the day before, climbing out of a cherry tree."

"And you worried about his lack of spirit."

"He's been a perfect angel the last few months. I should have realized that spelled trouble. This escapade is the first sign that he's still got the old imp inside him."

To his surprise—and pleasure—she slipped her hand through his arm. There was the usual jolt of male response, but with something sweeter and deeper flowing under it. Difficult to recall that he'd only met her last night. They talked like old friends.

"Perhaps he's coming to terms with losing his parents. I hate it when people talk about getting over a loss—you never do." Her voice was sad. "But life goes on regardless."

"You needed so much courage to carry on."

Her smile was self-deprecating. "I wasn't brave at all. I've hidden behind my widow's weeds since Waterloo. But early this year, two dear friends got sick of my moping and hauled me out of hibernation. We made a pact to be the dashing widows."

"The dashing widows? I like it. And I reckon you do yourself an injustice. Only the dashingest widow would take off into the night with a loudmouthed stranger."

She laughed as they descended the steps. He recognized that he was losing his head over this lovely—and dashing—widow.

"Put like that, I sound quite *outrée*, don't I? And I soon recognized that your bark was worse than your bite. At least when it came to me. It was patently clear that you were mad with worry."

"Carey's lucky he wasn't at your house. I wouldn't have been nearly so calm."

"Oh, you might have scolded him, but I doubt you'd have done much more."

They reached the ground floor and turned toward the morning room. The aromas of bacon and coffee reminded him that he'd been on the road all night. By now the sun was up and in the stark light, he saw the weariness on Fenella's remarkable face.

She paused in the doorway. "What a lovely room."

The morning room was decorated in the Chinese style popular last century, and its high windows overlooked a wilderness of garden, turned to enchantment with frost and early sunlight. Probert and two footmen arranged covered dishes on the sideboard.

Anthony stood beside her, ridiculously pleased at the praise. "Thank you. I thought we'd have breakfast here."

"I really should wash my travel dust off first."

Of course she must. Heat prickled the back of his neck. What a clod he was, not to offer her some privacy when they arrived. He nodded to a footman, who left to send up a girl from the kitchens. "I'll have a maid show you to a bedroom."

"And with your permission, I'll check on Mrs. Penn. I might be able to help. Also I'd like to send a note to London, letting the household know Brand's safe."

"You can spare half an hour to tidy up and have something to eat."

The warmth in her smile banished his awkwardness. "You're right. All that can wait."

A fresh-faced country girl came in and curtsied. "My lady, my name is Susan. I'll show you upstairs."

Fenella delayed to lay one slender hand on Anthony's arm. "Don't fret about Carey. You've both suffered an appalling loss, and you have a lot of adjustments to make. But love on both sides will smooth the way. You just need time to work out how to proceed. Kindness and patience will win the day."

Her eyes glowed as if she had every faith in him. Looking into her bonny face, he found himself believing her.

"Thank you," he said, wishing she'd keep touching him, but she left to follow Susan upstairs.

In a daze, he drifted across to sit at the round mahogany table, barely noticing when Gregory the footman placed a steaming cup of coffee before him.

He could blame his distraction on lack of sleep, or his overwhelming relief at finding the runaways. But he hadn't built his business empire from nothing by avoiding unwelcome truths. He wasn't going to start lying to himself now.

Unromantic, mundane Anthony Townsend was falling helplessly in love with a fine lady who, by rights, shouldn't spare him a glance. And he had no idea what in Hades to do about it.

CHAPTER SIX

It was late morning when Fenella emerged from her bedroom to check on Brand. A couple of hours of exhausted sleep had left her sluggish. As was often the way, she felt worse than she had when she'd rushed into the house at dawn, buoyed up with fear.

As she'd tidied her hair, she'd met shadowed blue eyes in her mirror. The night's travel had changed her in ways she wasn't yet ready to accept. The woman looking back at her was frightened to death that the firm ground beneath her feet turned to quicksand.

The boys' bedrooms were empty. With a clear if cold day, she guessed they must be outside somewhere. They wouldn't go far. Brand must be well aware a lecture awaited, and he'd never been a coward.

Unlike his mother.

Who hoped desperately that the intriguing Mr.

Townsend slept the day away. Then she needn't face the knowledge that while she was a mother, she was a woman, too. A woman who had been wrong to believe all interest in an attractive man died with her beloved husband.

When a footman told her the boys were with Mrs. Penn, she made her way to the east wing for the second time. Mr. Townsend provided generously for the woman who had cared for him as a baby. Unfortunately, not all the generosity in the world could change the sad reality that Carey's nurse was unlikely to live much longer. If Fenella had ever wanted to blame Carey for needless panic, one glance at Mrs. Penn's drawn face had told her he was right to rush to her side.

"Lady Deerham, how kind you are to check on me again," Mrs. Penn said when Fenella arrived. Her smile didn't hide her frailty.

Carey sat on the bed playing cards with her. Brand had pulled a chair up to the game and gripped five grubby cards in one hand. Marbles on the patchwork counterpane showed the stakes. At the moment, Carey was winning.

"Mamma!" Brand said, throwing his cards down and diving across the room into her arms.

"Oh, Brand..." With a muffled sob, she dragged him into a desperate embrace.

Immediately, the familiar little-boy smell of him soothed away the last remnants of her fear. Although he'd grown in the last month. Soon he'd be taller than she was. A sharp reminder that his precious childhood years were so short—and she was missing them.

After a moment's indecision, he hugged her back. But she understood masculine pride enough to know that he wouldn't appreciate his mother weeping all over him in front of his friend. After a kiss on his cheek, she reluctantly released him.

Brand stepped back and gave her an uncertain smile. "You're not pleased with me."

He was so infinitely dear and vulnerable, and she could so easily have lost him last night. But some instinct told her to play this particular scene lightly, not as the tragic, widowed mother. She knew he expected a well-deserved reprimand, but she was still at the stage where relief outweighed her urge to chide. "I'm happy you're all right."

She tried not to fret at the dark circles under his blue eyes. He was safe. That was all that mattered right now. His ill-fitting clothing, borrowed from Carey she assumed, sparked another rush of poignant tenderness. With bony ankles and wrists on show, he looked more like a street urchin than a young baronet.

"There was no harm done in the end," Mrs. Penn said.

"That's something my son and I are going to discuss at length later," she said in a steely voice, even as her hands itched to clutch Brand to her and never let him go. "I just want to make sure these two rascals aren't disturbing you."

"Three." Mrs. Penn tilted her head toward Mr. Townsend, standing solid as a huge tree near the window.

"Yes." Fenella glanced at Mr. Townsend—who disturbed her even if he didn't disturb his old nanny. He leaned one shoulder against the flowered wallpaper and surveyed the boys with wry amusement. He must wonder how all the mad fury of their chase through the night ended in this cozy scene. She wondered herself.

When they'd arrived at the Beeches, whiskers had darkened his already swarthy features, lending credence to her fantasies of him sailing the world as a swashbuckling sea captain. He'd since found time to shave, and change into a smart blue coat and buff trousers. Now he looked like a dashing, fashionable gentleman instead of a wild pirate.

Fenella was almost sorry.

She'd changed, too, into a rose pink morning gown —she blessed Greaves's forethought in packing that small bag. The idea of spending all day in the travel-worn blue carriage dress made her shudder.

"Nowt better than energetic young lads around the place." Mrs. Penn regarded the boys with exasperated fondness. "Even if these imps of Satan shouldn't have run away from school."

Carey's worried glance at his guardian encountered

a sardonic lift of one black eyebrow. With perfect composure, the boy returned to perusing his cards. Whatever else this escapade brought, Fenella was glad to see that uncle and nephew were well on the road to an understanding.

Carey had the look of his uncle. The same air of contained energy. The intense features, incongruous on a young face, although he'd grow into them. A body, like Brand's, that promised future height, but was all gangling awkwardness now. Compared to his friend's saturnine darkness, Brandon seemed brilliantly fair.

Mrs. Penn turned to her former charge. "And how grand to see you, too, Master Tony. This old house is too quiet and empty without the family. Young Carey caged in that den of iniquity, and you gallivanting on the high seas every hour the good Lord sends." She paused. "Especially with Mr. William and his dear wife lost to us."

Familiar sorrow flashed in his eyes. "You know I'd give anything to have them back, Penny."

The old woman brushed a skeletal hand over Carey's unruly thatch of hair so like his uncle's. "You two shouldn't grieve alone when you're all the family left to each other."

"Lads are sent away to school."

"Not in my family they're not—and you never had to go away either. The local grammar school was good enough for you. And for your brother. Most of the time, your brain works well enough to keep the wolf from the door."

He straightened and muffled a sigh, running his hand through his hair. Fenella found this interaction fascinating. This old lady had powerful Anthony Townsend at a complete disadvantage, despite his wealth, arrogance, and as Mrs. Penn pointed out, brain.

"Penny, Carey is growing up in a different world from the one I knew. As my heir—"

Mrs. Penn made a dismissive sound. "He won't be your heir for long. You'll marry and have bairns of your own."

"Carey will always have a place in my home," he said stiffly.

That tone cut no ice with this irrepressible old woman. Fenella wanted to cheer—and she liked Mr. Townsend even better for giving his old nurse a hearing when she didn't say what he wanted to hear. It was terrifying how much and how quickly she'd grown to admire this large, irascible man who concealed such unexpected sweetness in his heart.

"Of course he will. But right now, you two need each other, and you should be here together, not half a world apart." She sent Fenella a meaningful glance. "A man reaches the age when he needs the comforts of home. A fine house, a wife, children."

Fenella cursed that Mr. Townsend looked in her direction just then and caught her blush. It was her turn to undergo the eyebrow's inquisition. She glanced away to find Brand following the discussion with an intent expression.

Mr. Townsend turned back to Mrs. Penn. "Carey will grow up to take a place in the world—and boys who do that go away to school."

"Not always," Fenella found herself saying, despite reminding herself that this was none of her business. "Many children from good families are tutored at home."

Three pairs of masculine eyes settled on her in surprise and curiosity. "You never gave me any choice about school," Brand said slowly. "It was just accepted that I'd go."

She regarded her son searchingly. His tone as much as his manner alerted her to something going on beneath the surface. "It's what your father wanted."

"Was it what you wanted?"

"What I wanted didn't matter. It's what's best for you."

"So if the decision was yours alone, you wouldn't send me away?"

Dear heaven, where was this coming from? "I didn't send you away."

"Yes, you did."

She clenched her hands in her skirts as disquiet knotted her stomach. Her son had hidden his true feelings from her. Which hurt. And made her feel guilty. "I thought you liked school."

He shrugged. "It's all right. It's been better since Carey started."

She loathed to hear that he was miserable—and that he hadn't confided in her. "You never said anything."

"I didn't want to upset you." He looked startlingly adult, and she had a sudden, poignant vision of him as a man. "The way I've upset you now."

"Devil take you, lad," Mr. Townsend growled. "I won't have you worrying your mother."

When he stepped forward, Fenella caught his arm. Out of the corner of her eye, she noted Mrs. Penn's avid expression. "No, he's right to tell me. He should have told me before. Brand, I'm so sorry. Is that why you ran away?"

Brandon dipped his bright head and shuffled his feet, and returned to looking like an eleven-year-old boy. "No, of course not. I'd never be so craven as to run away just because I was unhappy."

Which meant he had been miserable. The guilt pierced deeper. How could she not have known?

"Come here," she said huskily. He shot her a quick grin and slipped under her arm. She hugged him close to her side, grateful all over again that he'd come out of his adventure in one piece.

Carey, who had remained a silent observer, scrambled to stand. "I told Brand I had to see Penny, and he said no true friend would let me go without someone to watch my back." When he smiled at the old lady,

Fenella's heart went out to the motherless child, so gallant, so fragile. "I had to come, Penny. You're family."

"You must have known I'd bring you down to see Penny if you asked me," Mr. Townsend said austerely. "By the way, how the hell did you get here so quickly?"

"Language, Master Tony," Penny said repressively. "There's a lady present."

The faint pink in his cheeks charmed Fenella, but he wasn't about to let Carey off the hook. "Well, young man?"

"I used my birthday money to pay Old Jock's nephew to take us."

"Did you indeed? And who, pray tell, is Old Jock?"

"He's one of the school gardeners. His nephew Fergus is first rate. You'll like him."

"I rather doubt it. Is he still here?"

"No, he had to get the cart back to Bray to take the piglets to market."

"So you see, we were never in danger," Brand said staunchly.

Mr. Townsend looked unconvinced. "You've worried your poor mother sick. You worried her so much that she trusted her safety to a stranger and sat in an open carriage all night. She didn't get a wink of sleep for fear of what might happen to you."

"It wasn't..." Fenella began, but faltered under his direct gaze. Because of course, it had been exactly like that. Her grip on her son tightened as she recalled how frantic she'd been for his safety.

Carey raised his chin, increasing his resemblance to his uncle. "I deserve a beating."

"Yes," Brand said with less conviction. Fenella had never raised a hand to her child, much as that had incurred Henry's mother's disapproval. He stepped out of her embrace, his jaw set in a stubborn line. "Although I did write to Mamma to tell her."

"Thank goodness you did," Fenella said. "We were about to call in the Bow Street Runners."

"Cor," Carey said.

"Young gentlemen do not say cor." Mr. Townsend narrowed his eyes at Fenella who was trying not to laugh. It had been difficult enough stifling a giggle at the idea of piglets taking precedence over a young baronet and his wealthy friend. "You're lucky this lunacy didn't end in disaster—I've no idea what the masters at Eton will say. You'll probably both be expelled."

"Good," Carey dared to say.

"Don't push your luck, young man," Mr. Townsend said in a quelling voice.

"You really don't want to go back to school, Brand?" Fenella asked.

Brand glanced at Mr. Townsend as if he had some say. A poignant reminder of the sad lack of a male authority figure in her family. "Do I have a choice?"

She spread her hands in bewilderment. "I don't know. You've hit me with this out of the blue. You know Creston Hall is tenanted for the next five years, so we can't go there. Your grandmother isn't up to looking after you in Bath." Henry's mother was hopelessly old-fashioned in her ideas, and she'd never recovered from her only son's death. "And while I'd love to have you in London, it's not a suitable place for a child."

"Brand could stay here," Carey chipped in.

His uncle subjected him to the sardonic eyebrow. "And where the deuce will you be while Brandon's settling into the Beeches, my lad?"

"You can't send the poor mite back to that nest of heathens," Mrs. Penn protested, looking unconvincingly piteous.

"Poor mite?" Mr. Townsend said drily. "A few minutes ago, you called him an imp of Satan."

"Can't I stay here?" Carey fixed burning dark eyes on his uncle. "Please?"

Mr. Townsend's lips flattened in frustration. "There's nobody to supervise you."

"You could get me a tutor."

"Not good enough. This latest mess only confirms that you need a firm hand."

"You've got a firm hand."

"I live in London."

"You could live here."

"Aye," Mrs. Penny said. "The house needs a master. And you must be sick of traipsing around all those foreign places."

"You think so?"

"You've got a boy to raise. His father wouldn't want the lad unhappy."

Mr. Townsend went ashen under his tan. It had been a telling blow—and the canny old woman knew it.

Carey still hadn't given up. Fenella admired his persistence, a quality he shared with his guardian. "Will you at least think about it, sir?"

Mr. Townsend nodded shortly. "I'll think—but that doesn't mean you've swayed me."

Carey's brilliant smile reminded Fenella of his uncle's charm when he forgot his sternness. "Capital, Uncle. And can Brand stay, too?"

"Brandon's mother won't like that."

Carey looked crestfallen, then cast Fenella a glance under his eyelashes. "Will you think about it, too?"

"Please, Mamma," Brand said.

"You can't saddle poor Mr. Townsend with the care of two unruly ruffians," she said helplessly. "Be reasonable, Brand."

An uncharacteristically mulish look settled on her son's face. "I won't go back to school without Carey."

"Brand…" she began in a warning tone.

"Apologize to your mother," Mr. Townsend snapped. "And while you're at it, tell her you're sorry for dragging her all the way to Hampshire in the middle of a freezing night."

Remorse filled Brand's face and he stepped forward. "I'm sorry, Mamma. I hope you'll forgive me."

"I'll forgive you as long as you promise never to do it again."

"I promise," Brandon said solemnly.

Carey approached his uncle and awkwardly stuck out his hand. "Will you forgive me, too, sir? I regret causing so much trouble, but my intentions were good."

When the two Townsends briefly shook hands, the tension drained from Carey's thin shoulders. For one resonant moment, the two stared at each other. Then the man tugged the boy into his arms.

"Come here, you appalling brat. Of course you're forgiven. Although when I found out you'd taken off from school, I wished you to Hades."

Fenella's eyes misted up at this awkward, heartfelt rapprochement, as Carey gave a choked laugh and wriggled free. "I'll wager you did, Uncle." He turned to give Fenella a creditable bow. "Lady Deerham, I apologize to you, too. The scrape was totally my fault."

Fenella cast Brand a mocking glance. "My son was perfectly capable of saying no. But as nothing too dire has happened, we'll let bygones be bygones."

"Thank you, Mamma," Brand said with a quick smile.

"Nicely done, my lads," the old lady said from the bed. Fenella knew her praise included Mr. Townsend.

"We should leave you to rest," she said, noting Mrs. Penn's pallor.

"It's been grand to see the youngsters. But..."

"But they're a handful. I know." Fenella turned to the boys. "Collect your winnings and come downstairs."

As the boys said goodbye to Mrs. Penn and rushed ahead through the door, she couldn't help smiling. Despite hints of future maturity, they were still such babies.

"They're good bairns. I'm right glad you're not going to punish them," Mrs. Penn said, collapsing back with a rattling gasp. Fenella crossed to close the curtains before the old lady stopped her. "I'd rather see the sky, my lady."

"Very well."

"Dr. Brown will be here this afternoon." Mr. Townsend bent to kiss his nurse's lined cheek with a touching lack of self-consciousness.

"He's an old fool," she grumbled. "Always prying and prodding."

"He speaks right highly of you."

Mrs. Penn gave a weary grunt of laughter. "Get away with you, lad, you and your nonsense. And make sure you show this bonny lady over the house. It's a fine place and if you impress her, she might decide to take you on."

Mr. Townsend burst out laughing and kissed Mrs. Penn again as Fenella, furiously blushing, said, "Mr. Townsend and I only met last night. You misunderstand."

Mrs. Penn's eyes fluttered shut, but a faint smile

curved her mouth. "Forgive a doddery old woman. My mind's not what it used to be."

Mr. Townsend took Fenella's arm and led her from the room, closing the door after him.

"She's a troublemaker," Fenella said.

He cast her an amused glance, and she marveled yet again how much more approachable he looked when he was laughing. "She is, at that."

"Does she try to marry you off to every unattached female she sees in your company? That must wear out its welcome."

He regarded her thoughtfully. "You know, this is the first time she's done that. You're special."

Fenella's dismissive snort would have shocked her swains in London, all of whom were convinced of her fastidious nature. "It must be her illness."

He raised that speaking eyebrow. "So you're brave enough to see through the house?"

Fenella responded with a speaking look. "I dare you to show me. I'll struggle to resist the temptation to drag you before the nearest vicar."

He gave a theatrical sigh. "You know the risks. On your own head be it."

Only as they descended the stairs did she realize that Mr. Townsend hadn't scoffed at Mrs. Penn's matchmaking. She hadn't realized he was so tactful.

CHAPTER SEVEN

After dinner, Anthony sipped his brandy and studied the lovely woman drinking tea on the other side of his drawing room. The lads had eaten with them, then retired with surprising docility which meant they were probably upstairs hatching mischief. Anthony couldn't get too exercised about the possibility when he had a bonny lass to look at, a blazing fire to sit beside, and a belly full of an excellent dinner.

Like everything else at the Beeches, the room was shabby, but with the potential for magnificence. A room in need of a woman's touch, in fact.

He wanted that woman to be Fenella Deerham.

He'd built an extravagant fortune on following his instincts. In this case, his instincts verged on madness. Her family pedigree stretched back to Adam. All his money couldn't match her aristocratic refinement.

And the highest barrier of all between them: she was still in love with her late husband.

For years, Anthony had kept a mistress, a widow of mature years, cheerful temper, and intelligent conversation, in a small house in Kensington. Eighteen months ago, she'd sent him on his way kindly but firmly, and had since married a ship's captain. He thought of Flora fondly, but without regret.

After Flora's departure, his bed had stayed empty. Too much else occupied his attention. His crushing burden of grief. His duty to Carey. A government clamoring for advice. Not to mention the demands of running a worldwide enterprise.

Then he'd found himself in a gallant lady's company, racing through the night in search of two runaway rapscallions. And his life had turned in a dazzling new direction.

Last night Fenella had cuddled up to him in the carriage's close confines. All day, tormenting little contacts had kept his blood at a constant simmer. If she was the sort of woman he was used to—earthy, practical, familiar with desire—he'd think she indicated interest.

But she was a blasted lady. He had no experience with that exotic species.

He couldn't imagine her fancying a hulking brute like him. And after they'd established such harmony, he balked at destroying their rapport with an improper proposition.

Dear Lord above, how he burned to make that proposition. There she sat, drinking tea and dreaming of sugarplums and daisies, or whatever the hell gentlewomen thought about. And all Anthony wanted was to drag her down onto the worn carpet and thrust inside her until she sobbed with release.

He'd had one victory at least. She'd suggested returning to London this afternoon, although she'd been white with exhaustion. Shamelessly he'd used Brand's need to rest after all the excitement to convince her to remain. Now she was here, he didn't want her to leave.

"Please, stop scowling at me, Mr. Townsend," she said lightly, freshening her tea. "Is the brandy not to your taste?"

He smiled. He'd smiled more in her company than he had since William died. She had magic, this ethereal creature. "What the devil are we to do with these two rascals?"

He kicked himself when his question brought a troubled light to her blue eyes. "I had no idea Brand didn't like school."

"He didn't want to worry you."

"But if I knew, I could do something about it."

"Will you send him back?"

"Not this term, at least. And that's assuming the school will overlook him running away. I'll have to bring him to London. But that's only a temporary solution."

"You could leave him here. At least until the holidays."

"You're not sending Carey back?"

"No. Like you, I'd rather he was here and content. At least for the moment. He's had enough sadness in his young life."

"I'm so glad."

Her approval made him happier than he'd felt when he'd banked his first thousand pounds. "Penny's right. Now I've got the lad, things need to change. Perhaps I'll retire and become a lazy country squire who rides to hounds all day and drinks half the night."

She released a short laugh. "Not you. You'll set to modernizing the house. Then the gardens. Then the estate. Your poor tenants won't get a moment's peace without you pounding on their doors, forcing new roofs and the latest plumbing upon them."

Anthony responded with a huff of amusement. "I've got a powerful fear of boredom, Lady Deerham."

"Are you seriously thinking of moving to the country?"

"Aye. I can run my business from here if need be— London is in easy reach, as we proved last night. That's one of the reasons I bought this house—it's close to Southampton and Portsmouth, too. I just didn't imagine I'd move in until it was up to scratch."

"It merely needs a little work."

"More than a little. And I don't fancy living here with the builders in."

After stewing over his nephew's welfare for months, it was satisfying to share his thoughts and plans with a sensible, warmhearted woman. The sort of conversation one would have with a wife.

Fenella would make a damned fine wife. If some chap could persuade her to look beyond her first husband.

She shrugged. "Everyone says you're as rich as Croesus. You could travel, or rent somewhere else, or go back to London."

"And Carey?"

"He could go with you." She paused. "Or stay with me, wherever Brand and I end up. Right now, I have no idea where that will be."

"You're brave to the point of recklessness to offer to take him on."

She made a dismissive murmur. "Brand would like it."

"So would Carey, but I don't want to saddle you with my family problems. Carey's already caused a world of trouble. You must curse the name Townsend."

An enigmatic smile hovered around her full, pink mouth. Her full, pink, *kissable* mouth. "I certainly cursed it when a great bear of a man ripped his way into my drawing room and howled abuse."

Heat prickled his cheeks. "I haven't apologized adequately. My behavior was unforgivable."

The smile deepened without really taking hold. "You've grown on me since then."

"Like mold on cheese," he said gloomily, setting his empty glass on the spindly table at his elbow.

She laughed, as he'd intended. "More like ivy on a wall."

It was his turn to laugh. "So will you let Brand stay here until you decide his future?"

She frowned. "I'm…I'm not sure that's a good idea."

He jerked as if she'd struck him. She'd have hurt him less if she had. He should have expected this—after all, hadn't the differences between them been as plain as a bloody pikestaff from the start? Even so, his voice was humiliatingly rough when he spoke. "I'm sorry, my lady. I presumed where I had no right."

Astonishment widened her eyes. "What on earth are you talking about?"

"There's no need to put your objections into words."

"There jolly well is. What do you think I mean?"

The moment he began his awkward explanation, he realized he'd jumped to unwarranted conclusions. His uncharacteristic sensitivity was another sign of how important she was becoming. "Carey is a working man's son, whereas Brandon's blood is bluer than your bonny eyes."

He'd glimpsed her anger before. Now it blazed like fire, fixing him in his chair as she rose, a tiny, gorgeous bundle of blistering fury. "I resent that. Carey is a fine boy, and I'm overjoyed Brandon has found a friend who is loyal, true and brave. Carey risked a lot to see Mrs. Penn, perhaps for the last time.

Yet still he did it. If that's an example of a working man's son, the country needs more of them." Her tone turned freezing. "I have my doubts about Carey's uncle, however."

Anthony stood up and loomed over her. "Most women in your position would—"

"I'm not most women," she said curtly, cutting him off as nobody these days dared. And bugger him if he didn't like it. "How dare you say I'm too blinded by privilege to note a man's genuine worth? And I'm not talking about how much money you've got stashed away in Child's Bank, Mr. Townsend."

He caught her arms before he remembered he had no right to touch her. "Then what the hell did you mean when you said Brandon shouldn't stay?"

She stared up at him, eyes blue as the sky. This time, it was her turn to blush. "Don't make me explain."

His grip tightened. "If you approve of Brandon and Carey's friendship, why shouldn't the lads stay here? I'll keep an eye on them. For God's sake, if you're unsure of my guardianship, you could stay, too. I'd certainly like that."

With a muffled sound of frustration, she pulled free. "So would I. Can't you see that's the problem?"

Guilt stabbed him. He'd felt bad enough when he thought she scorned his humble background. This was worse. He straightened. "You're afraid I mean to act dishonorably. You have my word, Lady Deerham. You're safe under my roof."

She exhaled with impatience. "Oh, how can a clever man be so stupid?"

"If I've made you feel uncomfortable, I can only apologize—again. I won't bedevil you with my attentions."

She made a nervous gesture. "I don't fear that. I'm not...averse to your attentions—and there lies my dilemma."

His mouth gaped in shock as she flushed with embarrassment. Her slender body vibrated with tension—or was it excitement?

"What...what did you say?" he finally summoned voice to ask, while his busy mind wrestled to make sense of her astonishing confession.

Because the obvious meaning couldn't be true in any universe Anthony Townsend inhabited.

She closed her eyes and sucked in an audible breath. "I'm not saying it again."

He spoke very clearly to avoid further misunderstandings. If he got this wrong, the consequences would be disastrous. "You're giving me to understand that...that you wouldn't object to a kiss or two?"

She stared at the floor, and her hands twined over each other in a dance of uncertainty. "It's impossible."

"Why?"

"Why?" Her eyes flashed up. "I'm a virtuous woman. And the scandal will be bad enough already, with me taking off into the night and staying unchaperoned in your house."

He smiled slowly. "We may as well be hanged for a sheep as a lamb."

She backed away. "You don't understand."

Actually he did. Finally. "You haven't had a lover since Sir Henry died, have you?"

"Of course not," she said hotly.

Vast tenderness flooded him, sweeping away hesitation. He'd wanted Fenella Deerham from the first. Discovering that she wanted him, too, emboldened him to meet all opposition head on. Even from a dead man.

"Fenella," he said gently, "you've been on your own for five years."

Distress turned her eyes glassy. He didn't underestimate the obstacles between them—the prospect of desiring someone new threatened to tear her apart. Let alone going on to do anything about it. "I love Henry."

"That's well and good. But you're a vibrant, attractive woman and, forgive my bluntness, you're here and he, God rest his soul, isn't."

"So I should leap into the bed of the first reprobate who shows an interest?" she asked bitterly.

Anthony couldn't help smiling. "I very much doubt I'm the first man in five years who's expressed his admiration." He inspected her thoughtfully. "But that's not the real problem, is it? The real problem is that I'm the first man who has aroused your interest in return."

"That's…that's why I think we should try and avoid one another."

He commended her courage—and honesty. His

laugh was wry. "That will be difficult if those two hellions continue to be best friends."

"We could try." Desperation edged her soft voice.

When he caught her trembling hand, the contact of skin on skin made her start as if he'd burned her. "Or we could see where this takes us."

She made a halfhearted attempt to pull away. "You mistake me. I don't want a lover."

"Why?"

She stared at him in helpless confusion. "I have a son to consider."

He smiled faintly and brought her hand to his lips. She gave another of those starts. "You're a woman with needs and feelings. Aren't you lonely, Fenella? Don't you miss a man's kisses, the touch of his hand, a warm body to cling to in the night?"

Not long ago she'd been pink as a sunset. Now she was pale as milk. "Stop it."

"No." His grip firmed. "Stay with me."

She stiffened and spoke in a cold voice. "I'm not going to your bed with my son in the house."

He smiled faintly. "I'm not expecting your capitulation tonight—however nice it would be."

"Mr. Townsend—"

"Anthony."

"*Mr.* Townsend, this serves no purpose. I'm sorry I admitted my…my penchant."

"I'm not."

Her eyes narrowed, although unwilling amusement

tugged at her lips. "It's like listening to your nephew wheedling to leave Eton. You're incorrigible."

"I'm enchanted. Stay and get to know me. Get to know Carey. Spend a few stolen days with Brand. I promise I won't put any pressure on you."

He saw she was tempted. "I can easily take Brand back with me tomorrow."

"Do you really mean to split the lads up, just because our attraction frightens you?"

"Emotional blackmail won't force me into your bed, sir."

"Anthony."

"And I didn't give you permission to call me Fenella."

"Lady Deerham is a prisoner of her sad past. Fenella, on the other hand, is warm and lovely and within reach."

"So call me Lady Deerham," she said crossly. "I see why you've succeeded in business. You browbeat your poor customers into submission."

"Does that mean you consent?"

She drew herself up and ripped her hand from his. "No, it means I'd appreciate the loan of a carriage tomorrow morning so I can return to London and do my best to scotch any talk."

"Will you leave Brand here?"

She regarded him uncertainly. "Common sense says it's best to sever all ties."

"So Brand pays the price for your cowardice?"

Her expression turned mutinous. "You're doing it again."

He spread his hands. "I need to use what weapons I have."

"No, you need to wave the white flag and surrender."

A pleased smile lifted his lips. "Ah, surrender is such a bonny word."

Her response was unimpressed. "I shall be frank, Mr. Townsend—"

"Anthony."

"*Mr.* Townsend. I shall be frank because you seem incapable of taking a polite no for an answer."

He snorted. "Polite?"

She ignored him and plowed on. "You're wasting your time pursuing me. I'm devoted to my late husband's memory. Please respect that and ignore my unwise admission of attraction. We met in unusual and dramatic circumstances. Neither of us really knows the other, and I suspect if we'd been introduced in a more prosaic setting, we'd find no particular affinity."

He bowed shortly. "You're brutally clear, my lady."

Fleeting regret darkened her eyes, but her delicate jaw set in a stubborn line. "I…I have no wish to change my life—however enticing the incentive."

He hid a smile. The ruthless tone hadn't lasted long. "I'll call upon you in London."

"Haven't you heard a word I said?"

"You said you mistrust any link formed in such circumstances. I acknowledge the justice of your doubts —and also that we've known each other a mere day. I shall endeavor to prove that we're attracted because of who we are, and not because we've had too much excitement."

She threw her hands up. "Oh, you're impossible. I'll be glad to get back to my real life."

"Will you?" he asked softly.

For a moment, she looked unsure, then her lush mouth firmed. "At least in Mayfair, I'm free of insane plutocrats and their persuasions."

He laughed, enjoying himself. "Yet."

He'd always intended to pursue her, but her confession of a weakness for him invited a more overt wooing. She was a grand little fighter, but he doubted she'd win when Anthony Townsend allied with her own desire against her.

"There's no point continuing. I'm tired, and you're off your head. Good night, Mr. Townsend." With an irritated swish of her skirts, she flounced off. He let her reach the door before he spoke. "Lady Deerham, there is one more thing."

"What is it?" Annoyance roughened her voice.

A man of his size could cross the room in a couple of paces. He caught her arm and using her surprise, swung her around to face him. A gentle push and her back bumped against the closed door. "This."

Furious eyes snapping blue fire focused on his face.

"Mr. Townsend, just what on earth do you think you're doing?"

"My dear Lady Deerham, surely it hasn't been that long."

"I'll scream," she warned, trying to slay him with her disapproval. Unfortunately for her, he found her spirit arousing. This close she smelled like a flower garden in spring. He drew that glorious scent deep into his lungs.

"I dare you." One hand pressed her shoulder against the door while the other caught her chin to hold her still.

Not that she was struggling. Which was dashed interesting.

"You are the most provoking man," she muttered.

"That's insane plutocrats for you." He hid a smile as anticipation made his blood rush. "Now stand still so I can kiss you."

"Well, really," she gasped before his lips stole her breath away.

CHAPTER EIGHT

enella's resistance dissolved in an ocean of wildfire. Everything was heat, strength, dominance.

Mr. Townsend crushed her against him while his mouth plundered hers. For too long, shock held her rigid. Then she made a muffled protest and struggled to push him away. He only growled deep in his throat and folded her closer into that big body.

She felt seized, conquered, compelled. And wickedly, unforgivably excited.

Her hands closed into fists and she beat on those wide, straight shoulders. When that didn't work, she pulled sharply at his thick, black hair and struggled to ignore its silky texture against her fingers.

He wrenched free and stared down at her with an appalled expression. His arms fell away from her. She sucked air into her lungs and prayed that her knees supported her. Her heart banged crazily against her ribs.

"Oh, hell, Fenella, I'm sorry."

She slumped breathlessly against the door, the oak hard against her back. As hard as Mr. Townsend's body. His rich male scent, brandy and sandalwood and clean healthy skin, teased her overstimulated senses.

"You…you shouldn't have done that," she said unsteadily.

She raised a shaking hand to lips that still burned. The kiss had lasted a mere sizzling second—although it had seemed an eternity. She'd forgotten the way huge, potent maleness could wrap around her and exclude the rest of the world. Although when it came to size and potency, Mr. Townsend completely eclipsed dear, loving Henry, the only other man she'd ever kissed.

The thought, however accurate, struck her as disloyal. Self-disgust straightened her backbone in a way nothing else could. "You didn't act like a gentleman."

"But then I'm not a gentleman."

She should be furious that he'd manhandled her, yet strangely, she wasn't. Perhaps because while he'd been masterful, he hadn't been rough. Which should be no excuse.

"I must go."

Except that her feet remained stubbornly glued to the floor. And Mr. Townsend remained far too close. Close enough for his warmth to entice her.

When Henry died, a great and eternal coldness had descended that not even her love for Brandon could vanquish.

Apparently the chill wasn't eternal after all. Cold was the last word to describe her reaction to that impetuous kiss. She'd never imagined she could feel like this again. She'd never wanted to feel like this again.

"Damn you, Fenella," he rasped. His body vibrated with tension, and he looked ready to fight an army single-handed. "If you're going, go. Or take the consequences."

Staring up at him, she flattened her palms against the door behind her. She should be terrified. But fear, like anger, proved elusive. Instead she was curious to discover if that immense strength could cherish as well as insist.

How brazen.

And dangerous. Mr. Townsend blazed with desire. She shouldn't encourage him. But dear heaven, that warmth drew her, reminded her that through nearly six empty years, no man had placed his hands on her in passion.

She shivered. His ferocious need was shamefully thrilling. Henry, for all his bravery as a soldier, had been the gentlest of men off the battlefield. Mr. Townsend looked ready to gobble her up with one snap of those strong white teeth.

He misunderstood her trembling silence. "After that

gaucherie, you have no reason to believe me, but you're safe."

"I know I am." She hardly recognized the reedy voice as hers.

His face, all harsh angles and hard male determination, filled with a tenderness that reminded her how careful he'd been with Carey. Even now, when he burned for her, he kept his hands off her.

Which suddenly struck her as a pity.

Misgivings receded under a wave of need. With breathtaking daring, she lifted one hand and laid it on his fine black coat above his thundering heart.

"Fenella? You're playing with fire."

"Oh, I do hope so," she murmured, stretching up on her tiptoes to brush her lips across his.

He didn't immediately react, so she did it again. Another disappointing lack of response, although a hum emerged from his throat.

Her skills must be rusty. She battled to recall what had once been so spontaneous. It had taken her so long to want to kiss a man again. She had no intention of retiring defeated.

Seeking a clue to how to approach him, she studied Mr. Townsend. He looked disgruntled and bewildered —as well he might, given the way she'd pushed him away after that first tempestuous kiss.

She sucked in a shuddering breath, told herself to be brave, and slid her hand up his chest and around that powerful neck. Tension turned the muscles under her fingers to rock.

Fenella stroked her other hand down his face, tracing the strong, austere bones. She'd forgotten, too, how fascinatingly different a man's body was from hers. And Anthony Townsend had struck her from the first as an uncompromisingly masculine man. She drew his head down and ran her lips over that obstinate jaw.

A muscle flickered in his cheek, and his breath emerged on a hiss. "Blast you, lass, you test me too far."

Implacable hands caught her waist. For a fraught instant, she wasn't sure if he meant to push her away or drag her closer. That strained, striking face told her he wasn't sure either.

He hauled her against him. She braced for another demonstration of male power.

But this kiss was different. His lips wooed and sipped and tasted. They requested her cooperation instead of demanding it. How could she say no? With a sigh, she gave herself up to him.

Fenella Deerham was as luscious as a ripe peach, as fragrant as a rose, as soft as new fallen snow. Anthony hungered to seize her and use her for his relentless enjoyment until they sprawled, wrung out and sated.

But even now, when she melted in wordless

consent, he wasn't a complete fool. Although he'd been close to completely witless since, instead of slapping his face, she'd launched a seduction of her own.

This was a woman to treasure, not commandeer.

So he eased his death grip on her waist—despite the urge to clutch her tight and never let go—and rather than ravishing her mouth, he played lazily with her lips. Little kisses. A stroke of the tongue too brief to threaten invasion. A nibble here. A nip there.

The storm inside him eased, and languorous pleasure became its own reward. The night and the rambling old house closed around them in soft embrace.

Anthony caught her head between his hands as he pursued his sensual discovery. The full lower lip. The precise cut of her upper lip. The indented corners. He dared a sweep of his tongue along the closed seam, provoking a quick gasp of breath, but didn't press his advantage. He felt like he had all the time in the world to gain a fuller surrender.

The kiss continued in sweet innocence. Although he'd had no claim to innocence since boyhood, and Fenella had known a husband's love. But still her kiss held a delicately untried quality. He recalled with a stab of indefinable emotion that this beautiful woman hadn't had a lover in over five years.

So his touch remained exploratory, rather than insistent, tender rather than passionate. However powerfully passion strained to break free.

"For pity's sake, Anthony, kiss me like you mean it," she gasped.

He gave a brief laugh and ran his lips down her throat, making her shiver. At last she'd called him Anthony—and without him asking. "Don't you like this?"

She made a wordless protest. "You know I do."

He commanded his hands to hold her lightly, despite driving need, as he scraped his teeth along the graceful curve where neck met shoulder. She smelled delicious there. Warm. Womanly. Needy. "So?"

She tugged sharply at his hair. His rose had thorns —he relished that hint of spice under all the sugar. "I'd like it more if you stopped treating me like I might shatter."

"Very well," he said and wrapped his arms around her. A step or two, and she lay flat under him on the chaise longue.

Blue eyes widened with shock. Now she knew exactly how much he wanted her. "Mr. Townsend?"

A wry smile twisted his lips. "I was Anthony last time."

"Perhaps…perhaps we should stand up."

He rose on his elbows. She was so delightfully ruffled and flushed, he couldn't resist another kiss. She spread beneath him like every dream come true. "I won't do anything you don't want me to."

She was clever enough to see the flaw in his offer. "That's no protection."

He frowned faintly. "Fenella, I swear I won't trespass beyond a few kisses. Despite wanting more."

"I knew this was a bad idea," she said shakily, fingers lacing through his hair.

"It doesn't feel like a bad idea."

Except, damn him, it did. If he had any claim to honor, he'd roll off her and exile her to her chaste widow's bed.

But he wasn't averse to taking risks—otherwise he'd still be running an obscure, not particularly profitable shipping firm. And while he was neither lunatic nor hopeful enough to imagine she'd surrender all at the first invitation, he wasn't ready to stop. Even if kissing her was an agonizing combination of delight and frustration.

This kiss was no longer teasing. It demanded that she counter Anthony's heat with her own. When his tongue traced her lips, Fenella opened in helpless pleasure. He tasted delicious, brandy and desire.

Sensations repressed too long overwhelmed her. Banishing the proper widow, and reviving the young girl, in love with her handsome husband. She'd forgotten what this sweet itch for a man's touch was like.

She remembered now. Dear Lord, how she remembered.

Except this was different. Perhaps five years of denying that ardent girl built this wild release. Or thirty-year-old Fenella was a more complex woman than the innocent who had pledged herself to Henry Deerham.

Whatever the reason, Anthony's kisses stirred a dark tide of response she'd never known. When she plunged eager hands into his thick hair to bring that seeking mouth closer, he released a grunt of surprise. But she was past false modesty or pretend reluctance. For the first time in five years, she had blood in her veins, instead of rivers of cold salt tears.

She tugged at Anthony's neck cloth until his shirt fell open. When her hand found hot, smooth skin, she made a sound of satisfaction. She nipped at his lips, then sucked his tongue into her mouth.

This was like magic. This was like flying. This was like…

Betrayal.

A stifled protest escaped her, and the embrace turned alien and unwelcome. This time, when she caught his shoulders, she didn't mean to caress but to deny. Although surely no man would heed her when only seconds ago, she'd lain in his arms, delirious with rising passion.

To her relief, Anthony shifted away. He stared down at her, eyes dark and heavy-lidded. Pleasure softened his rough-hewn features, giving him the look of a sleepy lion. "Fenella?"

Until Anthony—Mr. Townsend—had kissed her, she'd had no idea how desperate she was for a man's touch. Since losing Henry, she'd lived frozen but safe. Now the ice melted forever. She hated to be so weak. So demanding. So pathetic.

Her hands clenched against those broad shoulders and sick with shame, she closed her eyes. His legs remained tangled in her filmy pink skirts, and on the narrow chaise longue, she couldn't avoid the massive weight of his arousal.

"Please…let me go."

With a powerful surge, he rose to his feet. "Forgive me."

Shakily she pushed up against the back of the chair. Sliding her feet to the floor didn't help her feel any more grounded. Her heart still raced, her blood simmered, and her lips throbbed from his kisses.

Much as she'd like to blame him for her loss of control, honesty prevailed. "No. I should have stopped you at the door. I've behaved disgracefully. What must you think of me?"

Unexpected humor twisted his lips. "It's not as bad as all that, surely. You haven't murdered anyone, lass."

"I beg your pardon?" she stammered. Part of her wanted to bewail her lapse. Another part wanted to slap him. And one tiny element wanted to cling to that superb form and let his kisses find their natural end.

"No need." His cheerful smile made the urge to clout him paramount. "I had a thoroughly nice time."

She spluttered like an outraged dowager hearing an off-color joke. "I meant I must have misheard what you said."

He laughed and extended his hand. "I know what you meant. But there's no need for all this breast beating."

"I let you touch me."

"And you enjoyed it."

"I know," she said desolately, and without thinking curled her fingers around that capable, callused hand. It was a working man's hand, reminding her again how different he was from her London beaux. But those large, blunt fingers had their own grace—and breathtaking skill on a woman's skin.

"Be a mite kinder to yourself, Fenella. Succumbing to a moment's temptation doesn't consign you to the lowest circle of hell."

She stood on rubbery legs. It took a worrying effort of will to release Anthony's hand. Everything about him was so big and warm. Her deepest instinct was to cuddle up against him and let him protect her from the cold, nasty world. When right now, the greatest threat to everything she'd ever believed about herself was Mr. Anthony Townsend.

"You're remarkably jolly," she said in a sour voice.

He shrugged. "As you said, with the boys upstairs, we couldn't go too far."

"Oh, Lord," she breathed in horror. She'd completely forgotten Brand. What on earth was wrong with her?

She blushed when Anthony bent to retrieve the neck cloth she'd removed and cast aside.

He continued as lightly as if they'd just ended a casual hand of piquet. "All in all, it's a promising start."

"A promising start?" she asked on a rising note, hating that the dowager was back.

He opened the door. "I look forward to seeing where we go from here."

Her eyes narrowed as her spirit stirred. "From here, Mr. Townsend, I'm going back to London." She marched past him into the hall. "While you, sir, can go to the devil."

"You can't find your room," Anthony said softly, standing beside her in the cavernous space. It was a pity that Fenella's splendid exit ended with her staring in confusion at the staircase.

"If I ask you, I'll have to get off my high horse."

"Aye." He lit two candles from the branch on the ancient sideboard and passed one to her. "But I promise to contain my smugness until you're safely inside your chamber."

She regarded him doubtfully. "Perhaps you should call a maid."

"On my honor, you're safe. The lads are effective chaperones."

"You'll think my hesitation is absurd, given what we just did."

He offered his arm and to his relief, she accepted it. He'd already noticed she didn't hold a grudge. "I think you're entirely charming. Surely you know that."

His declaration troubled rather than pleased her. "You're very kind."

I'm very besotted.

What was the point of fighting? It was true. It had been true from the first. He kept the thought to himself and began to outline his plans for the house. By the time they arrived at her room, her smile was almost natural. "Thank you. I'd never have found my way."

"Sleep well, Fenella." He smiled back as he reached past her to open the door. Then because he couldn't resist, he kissed her gently.

In the flickering candlelight, he studied her bonny face. He saw signs of exhaustion and strain. And reluctance and confusion. A hint of guilt.

And deep in the blue eyes, a longing that called him as inexorably as the moon drew the tide. His heart kicked with futile excitement. After all, right now he couldn't do anything about it.

"Good night," she whispered. As she disappeared behind the door, he heard her murmur, "Anthony."

He stared at the closed door. Much as he burned to follow her into that room, now wasn't the time. His blood might beat with the primitive urge to conquer and possess, but he wasn't an impetuous boy. Every instinct screamed that if he pushed now, he'd lose any chance with her.

Fenella Deerham had ceded more than she wanted to. He must be satisfied with that—and hope that if he won her trust, she might yet give him everything.

First he needed to lure her back toward life. He didn't resent her love for her first husband—or no more than any man wanting a woman who still dreamed of another lover. He even found it in himself to be glad that she'd known a good man's love. She deserved it. Hell, she deserved everything good in the world.

But Deerham was dead. While Fenella was alive, and unless Anthony deceived himself, attracted.

Because the prize was worth winning, he'd proceed cautiously. But in this empty hallway close to midnight, he vowed to raise Fenella Deerham out of sorrow into the bright sunlight of joy.

CHAPTER NINE

Fenella sat squeezed next to Anthony in his sporty carriage. Night was falling, and they were still more than an hour from London.

She thought the journey down had been awkward. She'd had no idea. Now the big, warm body wasn't a stranger's—far from it, she knew so many intimate things about him, from the taste of his kiss to the scent of his skin—and she wished herself a million miles away.

"Damn it, woman, stop wriggling," he growled. "It's like being tied in a sack with a dozen eels."

"You didn't have to drive me," she pointed out, folding gloved hands in her lap to hide their shaming tendency to tremble.

"Aye, I do. If you're so all-fired keen to get back, I'll see you arrive safely."

He sounded grumpy. So did she. "We've risked enough scandal."

In the fading light, she saw his lips turn down in derision. "Then the damage is done. You might as well have stayed."

"You know I couldn't."

"I know no such thing. Brand would like it."

Brand would indeed like it. So, unfortunately, would she. The regrettable truth was that she'd fled the Beeches because she was afraid, not because she guarded her reputation.

"Brand got a fair share of what he wanted anyway, considering how much trouble he and Carey caused," she said grimly.

She'd given in to her son's pleading and left him behind. She couldn't send him back to school, whatever accusations of coddling that invited from her monumental companion.

Last night she'd gone to her lonely bed, determined to leave at the earliest possible moment. Yet somehow the morning had dwindled away in spending time with the boys and trying not to dwell on last night's kisses.

It had been a wrench to leave her son. It always was. Even now when they might find a way to live under the same roof. Perhaps this escapade would end happily for Brand at least. Except somewhere in the last twenty-four hours, the idea of a quiet, rural hideaway for Brand and her had lost its charm.

Curse Anthony Townsend and his kisses.

"You've forgiven them," he said. "You forgave them the minute you saw they were safe."

"So did you," she said, stung at the implied criticism.

A grunt of self-derisive amusement escaped. "I waited at least another five minutes."

Despite weariness and bad temper, she laughed. Odd how Anthony could do that.

She had no trouble diagnosing the root of his crankiness. She suffered the same malady. A bad case of sexual frustration. She'd lain awake all night, restless and longing for more kisses.

For more than kisses.

"You think they'll be all right?"

"I'm only away overnight, and the place is packed with servants—including Penny, who won't let them get away with any mischief, however ill she is. And they both know they've escaped lightly after their escapades. They're on their best behavior." He drew the horses to a halt under a spreading oak and faced her with a serious expression.

"What is it?" she asked, suddenly nervous. "Why have we stopped? Is something wrong?"

"I hope not." A wry smile quirked his lips. "I'd like to talk to you."

She frowned. "The boys."

He shook his dark head. "No. Not this time." He subjected her to a searching look. "I have a proposition."

Oh, dear Lord. She knew exactly what was coming.

Forbidden excitement shivered through her. "Mr. Townsend..."

For once he didn't object to the formal address. Instead he went on in a measured, *reasonable* voice, as if what he suggested wasn't purest madness. "You mention scandal, but nobody except the staff at the Beeches know where we've been these last days. Nobody at all knows where we are now. We're free in a way we won't be free once we resume our daily lives."

"Freedom doesn't mean license must rule." She twined her hands together as an army of elephants started capering in her stomach.

This time he smiled properly, and the elephants thudded down into a heap, before jumping up to start prancing again. That smile was a deadly weapon.

"Perhaps not, but it means if a virtuous lady felt the urge to...stray, she could do so without fearing gossip."

All the way from Hampshire, she'd cursed the carriage's close confines. Now it seemed as narrow as a child's pencil box. She gulped air into her lungs and wondered why she didn't slap this presumptuous cad's face and tell him to drive on. Or push him out onto the dusty grass verge and leave him to walk off his lust while she fled back to Mayfair and sanity. After all, she'd itched to take the reins ever since she'd first stepped into this stylish rig.

"You make too much of a moment's foolishness."

He surveyed her from under the curling brim of his stylish beaver hat. "Do I?"

Reluctantly she met that probing dark brown gaze, and saw that he already guessed most of her secrets. The most mortifying being that she wasn't virtuous at all, but starved for a man.

Not just any man. This one.

So instead of issuing a ringing denial, she responded in a quavering voice unworthy of a worldly woman past thirty. "I've…I've never done this before."

The tenderness that always proved so fatal to her resolve softened his eyes. "I know you haven't. I also know I've got a deuce of a cheek asking. You only met me two days ago, and it's clear you won't give yourself lightly."

No, she wouldn't. She'd shared her body with one man. Losing him had nearly destroyed her.

Anthony's offer belonged to a completely different world from her youthful adoration for Henry. But she had a sinking feeling that if she accepted this lunatic proposal, she wouldn't give herself lightly this time either. "You're making my arguments for me."

"Nor do I take this lightly. I wanted you the moment I saw you. That attraction has grown every moment since."

"Surely not." She strove to read his expression, but those rugged features didn't give much away. "You were furiously angry when we met."

"Angry, aye, but also attracted. It made for an uncomfortable mix, believe me. Now I find myself quite…desperate."

Still she examined that overtly masculine face. "You don't look desperate."

"I'm trying not to terrify you."

A wicked thrill rippled through her. The thought of testing this remarkable man's control was undeniably intriguing.

The horses snorted and stamped their feet, impatient at the delay. Sitting so close, she felt Anthony's vibrating tension. His face might be all stern angles, but his body hinted that he hung on her answer like a man dangling over a cliff.

She'd learned that with Anthony Townsend, you noted his actions, not his words.

What did they tell her? He loved his nephew, and had shown the two boys unexpected and poignant kindness. He was willing to admit his mistakes and take the consequences—in her experience, a rare and precious quality in the male animal. He possessed powerful appetites, but equally powerful control. Last night, he'd seen her resistance was precarious. But he'd let her retire unscathed. Almost.

Even now, he didn't touch her, to avoid influencing her decision.

So, a fair man. A man of principle. A man who could give her pleasure.

She'd always love Henry. She couldn't imagine sharing that closeness with anyone else. But that wasn't what Anthony offered.

He invited her to find fleeting surcease from loneliness, a sensual exploration, a brief warmth before she returned to the cold. That warmth lured most of all. To lie in a man's arms and feel her blood rise in passion, to accept physical comfort that asked for nothing more.

Ah, that was tempting.

She licked lips dry as the Sahara and quivered with uncertainty. And desire.

Heat flared in his eyes as they focused on her mouth. Yes, he wanted her. She couldn't doubt it. But did that mean she could trust him?

"What exactly is your proposition?" she asked huskily.

One of those large, expressive hands gestured to the road ahead. "In a couple of miles, we'll reach Croydon. I've taken a room at the Rainbow and Angel. We can spend the night. If not, I'll stay, and you can proceed alone to Mayfair in a closed carriage I've arranged for your use. You'll arrive home without anyone knowing you've been in my company since you left."

He'd devoted time, thought and money to her seduction. She wasn't sure whether to be offended or flattered. "So I have to decide now?"

He shook his head. "No. The carriage remains at your disposal all night. You don't have to do anything you don't want to."

He knew enough about her to realize that if he tried to corner her, she'd run. She began to see how he'd parlayed a small-scale shipping line into a global concern. He knew what he wanted. More importantly, he knew what other people wanted.

"It would be wrong to agree." She meant to sound resolute, but wanton longing roughened her words.

He shifted and stared hard at her. "Why?"

"You know why. I'm a respectable widow, and mother to a son who should be the reason for all I do."

Displeasure darkened his expression. "Hell, Fenella, it's unfair to Brand to make him the sole purpose of your existence. In the long run, he won't thank you for it. We share a strong attraction. Neither of us owes allegiance to anyone else. We have a chance to see what it could be like between us. A chance away from obligations and prying eyes." He paused. "After last night, aren't you curious?"

She prayed for guidance, but all she saw was Anthony's gaze burning into hers. Despite Henry and Brand and her good name, she so wanted to say yes.

"Fenella?" Her name emerged as a ragged gasp, proving his calm was all on the surface.

"I…"

A mail coach thundered by, and she angled away from the flying dust and the passengers' eyes. The world rudely intruded on the strange interlude of the last days.

Once the vehicle was out of earshot, she turned to watch Anthony soothe the horses, restive after the clattering interruption. She touched his brawny arm.

"Take me to the Rainbow and Angel, Anthony."

CHAPTER TEN

Fenella sat rigid with nerves as Anthony drove the carriage into the bustling inn yard. After hours of travel, she felt crumpled and dusty and not up to these elegant surroundings. She was also convinced that her imminent fall from grace was painted all over her. But the maid who showed her upstairs was deferential, and the room she entered wasn't the red bower of sin she'd imagined, but a well-appointed chamber with a view over the back garden, stark and bare with coming winter.

Anthony followed and set his hat on a table. "Still sure?"

With shaking fingers, she removed her bonnet and glanced around the room, partly from curiosity, but mostly to avoid his unwavering gaze. "No."

He laughed and gestured to a door she hadn't noticed. She hadn't noticed much. Her mind was too busy preparing for what loomed ahead. "If you need me, I'll be in the dressing room. I've ordered dinner. It shouldn't be long."

"Dressing room?" she repeated stupidly.

"We have a suite of rooms." He pointed to another door. "The bedroom's through there."

Oh, she was a henwit. "Of course it is."

A huff of self-derision escaped her. She should have realized that this was a parlor. There was no bed. The ridiculous thing about her jumpiness was that it didn't alter her decision to take Anthony as her lover.

He stepped closer without touching her. "Fenella, I meant it when I said you're free to decide what happens. We can have dinner, then drive on together to London. Or if you ring that bell, a servant will escort you to a carriage and you can travel home alone. Or you can sleep undisturbed in the bed, and we'll finish our journey tomorrow morning."

"You seem very familiar with this inn."

He gave that oddly endearing grunt of amusement. "Rein in your rioting imagination. I've never brought another woman here. It's sometimes a convenient place to break my journey to the Beeches. You're not the first lass to take my fancy. But I'm far from a rake. I work too hard to have time to pursue an endless parade of women."

"I'm being a goose, aren't I?" she said, not surprised he'd discerned the doubt prompting her remark. He was always quick to see beneath her surface. A quality that right now struck her as unnerving rather than appealing.

When he cupped her cheek, she felt the tenderness to her toes. "A lovely goose."

He brushed his lips across hers. The kiss was a promise of what was to come, and a reminder of last night's caresses. Her fears ebbed. In their place, a hint of sensual anticipation swirled through her blood.

A smile lit his dark eyes. "There should be hot water in the bedroom. I'll tidy up and meet you in here for dinner. No need to hurry. We've got all night."

And with that her fears, momentarily soothed, flared again.

After dinner, Anthony stood in the dressing room and met his troubled dark gaze in the cheval mirror. The stupidest fellow in England could see that Fenella was still skittish. He sighed, wishing she threw herself into this arrangement as wholeheartedly as he did.

Although what the hell else did he expect? They weren't far removed from strangers, and she still mourned her husband.

Ever since she'd agreed to share his bed, he'd burned to sweep her up in his arms and show her how much he wanted her. Making the offer, he'd been half convinced that she'd say no. But to his astounded joy, she'd consented.

All evening, she'd maintained a brittle composure. The effort she needed to bolster her courage, while admirable, was far from flattering. He had the unwelcome impression that she approached tonight like some foul-tasting medicine. Necessary, but unpleasant.

Now it was late, and she was still here. He merely needed to leave the dressing room, cross the parlor, and knock on the bedroom door.

Standing before the tall mirror, a vermilion silk dressing gown covering his nakedness, he admitted the stark truth. Tonight mattered because Fenella mattered. More than any woman before, and he had a bleak suspicion, more than any woman to come. What happened between them in this inn set the course for the rest of his life, good or ill.

He turned away from his reflection. Usually when embarking on a new venture, he knew exactly where he headed. Fenella had him in such a spin, he couldn't tell which way was up.

All he knew was that he wanted her more than he'd wanted anything in his life.

At Anthony's knock, a quiet word invited him into the bedroom. Carefully he eased the door open, like a mortal entering an enchanted kingdom.

In awed silence, he stopped on the threshold. For a long time, the only sound in the room was the fire crackling in the hearth. His head was swimming before he realized he'd forgotten to breathe. He sucked in a great gust of air and struggled to say something coherent.

"You're the most beautiful woman I've ever seen." The reverent whisper resonated like a vow.

Her lips, pink satin, curved in a smile. "Thank you."

In the firelight, she was exquisite. Rich gold hair tumbled around her shoulders—what a glorious privilege to see it unbound. She wore a sheer white nightgown, and as she stepped forward, the way it clung and flowed around her slender body set his unruly heart cartwheeling.

She stopped about a foot away and fixed eyes brimming with mystery and shy passion upon him. "I want this, Anthony. When I'm with you, I don't feel lonely anymore."

"Oh, Fenella," he said, moved by her confession. He set his hands around her waist, reveling in her slim strength, and drew her up for his kiss.

After last night, her eagerness was familiar, but the freedom in her response was new. His tongue swept into her mouth, and when she greeted him without hesitation, animal hunger jolted him. He buried his hands in the luxuriant hair and angled her face up for a kiss of unabashed carnality. She followed where he went, until the unforgettable moment when she thrust her tongue into his mouth and a hum of enjoyment emerged from her throat.

Anthony backed her toward the bed. Fenella was a creature of light and fire. Not afraid, but his equal. He loved that. Although in the last few days, the differences between them had mattered less and less, and what counted now was that he was a man in thrall to a woman, and that woman wanted him back.

He couldn't mistake her desire. Her greedy hands explored his chest and shoulders, bunching the silk against his skin until the dressing gown crumpled to the floor.

Her eyes devoured him with considerably more enthusiasm than she'd shown for the excellent dinner he'd watched her pick at. "Mr. Townsend, you are magnificent. I'm quite overcome."

Her blatant sensual interest—and admiration—filled him with pride. He loved that his big, muscular body pleased her. He'd feared she'd recoil from his size and vigor.

But he couldn't mistake the avid hunger in her eyes. Or in her touch as she flattened both hands on his broad chest with its thatch of black hair.

"Mmm," she murmured appreciatively.

Hell, these throaty murmurs tested his control. His cock, hard and erect, twitched. He clenched his hands in the flimsy lawn covering her hips, as he fought the urge to push her down and plunge into her.

"I'm very large," he said, almost in apology.

She bit her lip in hesitation, then to his astonishment, her glance fell to his dick, stiff and heavy and insistent. "Yes, you are."

His heart crashed to a stop when she slid one of those soft *lady's* hands down his belly, setting every muscle jumping. And curled her fingers around him. "Lucky me."

Despite the dizzying heat, a growl of amusement escaped. "No, lucky *me*."

He caught her hand and pressed his lips to those fluttering fingers. "I want to see you."

When he kissed her lips, her fevered enthusiasm made his blood pound. Reluctantly he raised his head. She was as addictive as wine. Her face was flushed and lovely, and her expression spoke surrender. But for all her boldness, he caught a shadow of earlier shyness.

"You're a gift," he murmured.

"Then pray, unwrap me," she whispered.

How he delighted in these hints of saucy humor. Carefully he gathered the nightdress in his hands. Slowly he slid it upward, knuckles brushing smooth, still unseen skin over thighs and hips and flanks. With a sudden tug, the garment was over her head and on its way to a distant corner. He caught her supple waist and lowered her to the bed.

Urgency rang through him like a volley of trumpets, but he delayed long enough to snatch an incendiary glimpse of her. Nothing in his heated fantasies matched the pure white perfection of Fenella Deerham, lying bare and impatient for his possession.

She was all long, lissome lines, stronger and leaner without clothes than she looked in her fashionable gowns. Slim grace, subtle curves, high pointed breasts shaped to fit his hands.

He came down over her, supporting himself on one arm while his hand began a wanton exploration. Her skin was soft and smooth, and the color of new cream. He cupped one delicious breast, and his thumb brushed the beaded pink tip.

As her nipple tightened to a pebbled raspberry point, her eyelids flickered down and her breath escaped in jagged gasps. In a plea for more, she moved restlessly on the sheets.

Slowly, although his craving built like a great crescendo, his hand drifted down her flank to her hip. She was shaking. So was he.

She rolled toward him and pressed her hot face into his chest. Her hands ran up and down his arms. Husky murmurs spurred him on. His hand trailed down to her buttocks, then around to part her thighs.

He stroked her slick cleft, tracing the secret valleys and rises. Her musky, female scent intoxicated him. With a shuddering gasp, she shifted onto her back to offer him access. Again he marveled at her generosity. When his thumb found the hard little knot of her pleasure and she jerked in response, he set out to tease and arouse.

She tautened under his caresses and when he slid one finger, then two into her, she whimpered. Gently at first, then with increasing urgency, he worked her. The needy clench of her muscles around his fingers threatened to blast him to ash. His balls tightened to the point of agony, but still he lingered to ensure her readiness.

She'd waited so long for a lover's touch. By God, he'd make the wait worthwhile, or his name wasn't Anthony Townsend.

He bent to take one pink nipple into his mouth. Flicking with his tongue, scraping his teeth over the sensitive peak, until she cried out and raised her hips to meet his seeking hand.

After an interval of delightful torture, she dug her fingers into his hair and pulled until she had his attention. With the salty taste of her skin tangy on his tongue, he looked up.

"Don't wait." She ran her fingers through his hair. "I want you so much."

"I want you, too," he murmured. How profound the simple words became when spoken to the right woman.

He angled himself up and kissed her. She made a discontented sound against his lips and deepened the contact, but he pulled away.

Anthony was in such a lather to be inside her, his control shredded to tatters. He was sharply conscious of his proportions, and he feared hurting her, despite her ardor. Gently he spread her legs and, using his hand to guide his entry, slid inside her.

Dear Lord, she was tight. She panted and dug her fingernails into his bare shoulders until he felt the sting. The hell of it was, he wasn't sure he could stop. Not now, poised on the edge of bliss.

His balls burned to complete the joining. Every muscle coiled until he feared he'd explode like an overheated chestnut in a fire. His heart pounded so ferociously, it must rattle the windows.

Fenella tugged at his hair again. Given her dreamy expression only moments ago, her uncompromising stare surprised him. "Anthony," she said clearly. "I won't break."

"What the devil?"

Her hands framed his face, and she stretched up to kiss his mouth with an unfettered eagerness that threatened to blow his head off. "I appreciate your consideration, I really do."

"That's good," he said doubtfully. By God, it was difficult to talk and rein in his ravenous urges at the same time. He was close to forgetting that she was lovely and refined—and unused to great brutes heaving about on top of her.

"But you're driving me mad with frustration," she said.

"I don't want to hurt you."

The softness in her eyes set his heart thumping in a whole new rhythm. "You won't hurt me. I've done this before. Remember?"

"Not for a long time," he mumbled, and despite his most valiant efforts, his hips jutted forward.

"Far too long." She kissed him again, briefly but with devastating effect. "It's unkind to make me wait any longer."

"Fenella…" he began, but she arched up on a sigh of surrender and this time, not even the end of the world could stop him taking what he wanted.

On a groan of helpless delight, Anthony thrust deep and felt her open in fervent welcome.

CHAPTER ELEVEN

enella felt like she started out on a long journey that stretched beyond this large, comfortable bed into infinity. But this first step? Ah, this first step was marvelous. She stretched beneath Anthony, basking in the snug fit of their bodies.

When he'd pushed inside her, he'd pressed his face into the curve of her neck. Now he raised his head and shifted, setting off delicious little explosions inside her. "Good?"

She smiled and twined her arms around his back, tracing his long, straight spine and the sleek muscles. "Better than good."

He kissed her, then tautened his hips and moved. The glide of his body drew a shivery sigh of enjoyment from her. A moment's emptiness before he filled her again.

Joined like this, she thought she'd never feel cold again. "More," she whispered, tilting up.

Her encouragement unleashed his power. His dark eyes turned blind, and he began to move with great, deliberate strokes, deep and high so she shuddered with each thrust.

She loved every moment. While she'd thrilled to his tenderness, she'd feared he meant to treat her as too fragile for genuine passion. But this possession spoke to her strength and stirred a turbulent reaction she'd never known.

Craving the end that turned her blood to fire, she shifted restlessly. But still he kept her teetering on the edge of release until she sobbed with frustration.

"Stop torturing me." Sweet, biddable Fenella Deerham fisted her hands and pounded on her lover's back to make him obey. He laughed breathlessly and with a surge of movement, rolled onto his back until she straddled him.

"Oh," she gasped, instinctively leaning forward to flatten her hands on his heaving chest. The crisp hair tickled her palms, and his skin was hot as a furnace. "I'm not sure…"

He caught her hips, keeping her in place before she scrambled away. "You haven't done this before?"

He sounded surprised. It seemed mad to blush when she was stark naked and Anthony was deep inside her, but this position seemed so outlandish as to be perverse. "Ridden a man like a horse? No, I most certainly have not."

The sweetness in his smile almost vanquished her jitters. "Try it. You'll like it."

"I don't think so." Fenella squirmed with discomfort.

Except when she moved, discomfort wasn't the result. A lightning jolt of pleasure blasted her, and she cried out in astonishment.

Anthony's smile was smug, as with a hitch of his hips, he touched parts of her she hadn't known existed. The spark ignited into cascading fire. Even as she told herself she couldn't possibly be so wicked, she wriggled again to summon those breathtaking sensations.

His hands tightened, and his lips drew back from his teeth in an expression of fierce delight. "Oh, aye, lass."

She couldn't complain about the view. Spread beneath her, he looked quite glorious. His olive skin gleamed like satin, and his superb physique showed to advantage against the crumpled white sheets.

"No need to look so pleased with yourself," she muttered, pressing down to ignite that quaking reaction once more.

"It's your turn to torture me." He squeezed her breasts, teasing the nipples to aching points until she writhed. With every second, she was less shocked and more curious.

"I don't know what to do," she confessed, embarrassed.

"Here." He caught her hips again, lifting her, then bringing her down in a sensual slide that set every nerve in her body alight. At this angle, he filled all of her.

"So I really do ride you?"

Odd how freely she asked the question. In bed with Henry, much as she'd liked what they'd done, she'd always been circumspect. But Anthony Townsend awoke a new Fenella. The new Fenella, despite earlier misgivings, very much liked this variation on mating.

"You really do."

Experimentally she imitated the movement he'd demonstrated and watched his expression reflect her enjoyment. What had seemed so unacceptable became more natural. With a smothered moan, she began to rise and fall over him, more like waves on the ocean than a rider.

His gaze focused on her bobbing breasts, and the unabashed hunger in his eyes made her feel like a goddess. She'd never imagined she could lead with a lover, dictating pace and rhythm. To her surprise, she liked it.

Daringly, she clenched on the descent. Anthony's groan was long and guttural. "Damnation, you drive me out of my mind."

She laughed with brazen abandon, and just because she could, tightened again and rolled her hips. He closed his eyes. "You'll kill me."

"Not yet." She shook her hair back from where it clung to her heated skin. "I'm not finished with you."

"Witch," he whispered, and caught her shoulders, sweeping her under him and thrusting deep.

She bowed up until her breasts crushed into his chest, then gasped as he moved more intently. For what felt like hours, she'd hovered close to shattering. Now craving spiraled higher with each slide of his body.

She dug her nails into his sinewy back and gasped for air. Then for one dizzy second, she balanced on a pinnacle of bright torment. Before in a flash of searing light, she tumbled over into purest ecstasy.

Mindlessly she clung to Anthony as she rocketed through incandescent space. She cried out at the wonder of it all, then again when finally his control broke and he drove into her, flooding her with his hot seed.

After the wild flight reached its breathless end, peace washed over her like a warm sea. Fenella collapsed back upon the bed in exhausted, trembling, joyful satiation.

Anthony stirred and opened his eyes to darkness. Since he'd plunged into a dreamless sleep with Fenella in his arms, the fire had burned down to embers. Limp and exhausted, she still snuggled against him.

She'd been remarkable, a miracle, beyond his most

extravagant fantasies. Now he wanted to do it all again. His cock rose against her belly and he rubbed languorously against her softness. She made a sleepy, incoherent murmur and turned toward him with an immediate trust that touched his soul. She leaned in to brush a kiss over his heart.

He rose over her, kissing her face, then very gently her lips. She gave another bewitching murmur and lifted her knees to cradle him between her thighs. He wasn't even convinced that she was awake, but her willingness was clear.

God knew, he was more than ready.

He slipped his hand down to stroke her. She was wet and hot, and at the touch of his fingers, she gave one of those little hums of pleasure that had so tantalized him last night.

Gradually, savoring every luscious sensation, he slid inside her. When she immediately tightened to bring him closer, his heart dissolved. The urgency that had marked their first explosive union was absent. In its place was a poignant need to cherish. He kissed her again, then started to move with a relentless gentleness that had her sighing in greeting every time he stroked deep. This was like floating on clouds of joy.

He kept up the careful rhythm as long as he could, but eventually, inevitably hunger rose. She quivered on a peak of satisfaction, less tempestuous, but slower and longer than before. He buried his face in her shoulder and groaned as he filled her. This joining was breathtakingly profound, for all the thunder and lightning of their first time.

Anthony sighed and rolled onto his back, shaping her to his side. She murmured again and curled against him, all relaxed, womanly satisfaction. As he idly stroked her tangled hair, he smiled to realize that despite what they'd just shared, she was still closer to asleep than awake.

He settled more comfortably against the pillows. Life offered a man nothing finer than a cozy bed on a cold night and his woman dozing in his arms. He didn't know what he'd done to deserve this happiness, but he meant to hold on to it. And to Fenella.

She shifted again and pressed a drowsy kiss above his heart where she'd kissed him before. The instinctive tenderness made his heart cramp with unfamiliar but devastating emotion. He'd never felt like this before. She shook his world to its very foundations.

Cuddling up again, Fenella brushed her cheek against his chest with open affection. She hadn't spoken at all when he'd been inside her, although her moans and sighs had been the sweetest of music. Now, her voice emerged thick with sleep.

"Oh, Henry, my darling, I love you so much."

CHAPTER TWELVE

nthony cracked open heavy eyelids to find Fenella Deerham on the window seat, staring outside into the dawn. She wore the blue traveling gown that had become so familiar.

After her tender declaration of love, he'd stayed awake for hours, staring at nothing. But eventually he must have dropped back to sleep. Not long ago if his gritty eyes were any indication.

She looked beautiful. She always did. And desperately sad.

That was no surprise. He wasn't exactly on top of the world himself. Despite a night of the best sex he'd ever had.

Anthony wasn't entirely sure how he felt about Fenella vowing her love to another man while she lay in his arms. Probably he should be angry, but she'd never hidden her allegiance. He was definitely hurt.

Moving inside Fenella, he'd felt closer to her than to anyone in his life. It was like they shared the same breath.

The sting of discovering he was as prone to romantic illusion as the next man lingered, much as he told himself to grow up and get over it. After all, she'd made no promises, least of all eternal devotion.

The problem was all his, damn it. Because somewhere in the last two days, his immovable, stubborn soul had set itself to win Fenella Deerham.

Who was still in love with a dead man.

And given her steadfast heart, always would be. That left Anthony wanting to rampage around like a wounded bear and break things.

When she looked toward the bed, the ache inside him sharpened to agony.

"You've been crying," he said austerely.

She wiped her cheeks with shaky hands. The childish gesture roused a poignant tenderness he had no idea what to do with. "You're awake."

"Aye." He pushed up against the pillows and regarded her from under lowered brows. "I'm sorry I made you cry."

She shook her head. "I was dreaming of Henry. I often do, but...last night it was like he was with me."

He winced at her honesty. That primitive urge to create mayhem strengthened, but he beat it back. It wasn't Fenella's fault that she wanted someone else. A temper tantrum from a man she saw as a fleeting presence in her life wouldn't change that. "I know."

She looked baffled. "How on earth do you know that?"

He shrugged and stared moodily across the room at the dead fire. What an apt symbol for what lay between him and Fenella.

Except his fire wasn't anything like doused. He still wanted her like the very devil.

"You talk in your sleep."

A blush colored her cheeks, so she looked about sixteen, instead of like a woman who had married and borne a child and lost her beloved husband. She must have looked like this when she'd married Henry. Lucky dog.

"I'm sorry," she said, with a poor attempt at lightness. "That must break some rule against mentioning former lovers in the presence of your current one."

He didn't respond. It was too excruciating to wonder if she'd ever suspected that the man making love to her in the early morning hours was Anthony and not her husband's ghost. Instead he asked a question, even if he knew the answer. Sod it. "So what happens now?"

To his surprise, she didn't announce her intention to have nowt more to do with that lovelorn lout Anthony Townsend. Instead she settled troubled blue eyes on him. How he hated to see the spiky lashes and pink eyelids. "What would you like to happen now?"

He straightened his legs under the sheets, folded his arms over his bare chest, and spoke words that until now he'd never linked together. "I'd like to marry you."

She paled and recoiled against the windowsill. He supposed that was answer enough. Self-derision tightened his lips as pain stabbed deep.

"That's mad."

He shrugged again, determined to lay his cards on the table, however hopeless his cause. "It might be, but nevertheless it's true. I want you in my life. I want you in my bed. With everything legal and aboveboard. You're not made for romantic intrigue. And we have the boys to consider."

She frowned, not in displeasure he thought, but because his offer puzzled her. "Is it because of my aristocratic connections?"

He laughed without amusement. "Not likely. You're enough of a prize on your own. You're clever and sensible—most of the time. You were reckless in the extreme setting out with a stranger in the middle of the night for parts unknown. But fear had turned your mind. And you're damned decorative. A pretty wife never goes amiss when a man has his way to make."

"Thank you," she said drily.

He straightened the sheet over his hips and wondered how he could sound so calm when such a storm raged inside him. "My interest in you is personal. Believe me, my fortune gains plenty of friends in high places. A stickler or two might object if I wanted to marry one of their daughters, but I'm widely accepted otherwise."

"How do you know about the daughters?" she asked sharply.

"Actually I don't. I imagine my gold might make up for lack of breeding, if I pushed the matter and the girl was willing. But don't imagine I run around proposing to all the stray gentlewomen I stumble across."

She didn't look particularly gratified. "What about women who aren't gentlewomen? How many of those have you proposed to?"

If he hadn't heard her declare her love for another man, he might think she was jealous. "You're the only woman I've asked to become my wife."

"I'm…flattered." She paused. "Although technically you haven't asked me."

He stared broodingly at the foot of the bed, wishing she was in his arms and not on the other side of the room. Wishing that when she dreamed, she dreamed of Anthony Townsend and not dead Henry Deerham. "What's the point? You won't have me."

To his surprise, she surged to her feet and glared at him with disapproval. "I never thought you so poor spirited. Why on earth wouldn't I have you?"

He jerked his head up and stared at her uncompromisingly. "Well, will you?"

With a sigh, she slumped back onto the window seat. "I don't know."

He supposed it was better than a flat refusal, even if it didn't feel like it. "Last night you said you loved me."

Shock flooded her face. "What? Really? I can't..." One hand made a sweeping gesture as if to point out the impossibility of his claim.

His lips twisted. "You kissed me and told me you loved me. Then you called me Henry."

A fraught silence crashed down, then her face crumpled in distress and he cursed himself for telling her. "How awful for you."

He hadn't thought she'd see his side. Her empathy didn't solve anything, but still his wretchedness eased. "Not what a man wants to hear after a trip to paradise."

Pink tinged her cheeks. "Oh, dear, I owe you an apology. I told you I was dreaming of Henry. And...and that was what I dreamed." To his surprise, she mustered a faint smile. "It was a very nice dream, if that's any consolation."

"Not much," he said gloomily.

"I can't imagine it is." She stared down at the hands linked in her lap. "After all, you have your pride."

He ground his teeth. "Hell, Fenella, you're still in love with your husband."

"Of course I am," she agreed softly.

"Well, there you have it, then," and hated that he sounded like a sulky child denied a treat, when he felt like she'd struck a mortal blow.

Another silence descended, prickling with all they'd shared over the last eventful days. When he glanced up, she watched him with an unreadable expression.

"Except you don't," she said, as if there had been no pause.

He frowned. "I don't understand."

"I loved Henry from the moment he came to my eighth birthday party as an overly superior twelve-year-old boy. He took a couple of years to catch up with me and see that we belonged together. So he was sixteen before we decided that we'd marry. And we did, five years later. I've never been interested in another man."

Anthony struggled not to resent her husband. It was hellishly difficult. "You don't need to give me the details."

Her smile was indulgent. "Perhaps not, but you're missing the point."

"I know you'll always love him."

"Yet within two days, I went to bed with you."

"We're in the grip of May madness," he said sourly. "In November."

A long-suffering sigh escaped her. "You're usually quicker than this. Don't you see?"

"See what?"

"I'm incurably faithful. I've never looked at anyone else. Because of Brandon, I have to be careful of my good name. Yet you asked, and I tumbled right into your arms. I'd say I'm suffering more than a passing attraction."

His heart rose. He could work with that. With sudden purpose, he left the bed and strode toward her. Discussion just muddied the waters between them, whereas when she lay beneath him, everything turned clear. "Then come back to bed."

She sighed again and briefly closed her eyes. "You're such a man."

"Of course I am." He scratched his chest and stretched luxuriantly. "I suspect you like that."

Her attention drifted south and his cock responded predictably. Her lips quirked. "Sometimes."

After last night, this bawdy side to proper Fenella Deerham shouldn't catch him unawares, but it still came as a charming surprise. "Only sometimes?"

She waved a dismissive hand and stared over his head. "Please stop parading around in all your glory. It's distracting me."

He sighed, but bent to collect the dressing gown from where it had fallen last night. He shrugged the heavy silk over his nakedness. "I know we need to sort things out. I know we have important choices to make. But we don't have to reach decisions about the rest of our lives this very minute. I'll get Carey and Brandon settled at the Beeches with some regular supervision, and I'll come up to London to court you—unless you find the idea intolerable."

"You know I don't."

Excellent. At last he approved of the discussion's direction. "I hoped. But this minute, we've got a room to ourselves and nobody will know what we do in it." He tilted one hip against the base of the bed. "And I have a powerful hunger. One night wasn't enough."

She bit her lip, and he caught a pleasing flicker of interest in her eyes, before to his regret, she shook her head. "I'm confused enough already."

"Really?"

"Really." She smoothed her blue skirts over her lap. "I'm sorry, Anthony."

"So am I," he muttered, daring to approach her. Her brittle quality made him fear that if he wasn't careful, she'd crack like fine porcelain overfired in the kiln. "What do you want me to do? I gather you've hatched some plan in that busy mind of yours."

Somber eyes studied him. That brief moment of lightness might never have existed. "It's been a mad few days. The boys running away. Meeting you. Our journey to Hampshire. What...what we did in this room."

He sat beside her and studied her. What he saw made every muscle clench in horrified repudiation. "Good God, Fenella, you're not sending me on my way forever with a fond farewell and no intention of ever seeing me again, are you? Have I really made such a mull of this?"

Her expression wasn't encouraging. "That seems the sensible option."

He caught her hand and struggled not to crush it in his desperation to convince her. "You've been sensible for five years, and all you've got to show for it is an empty bed and a lonely heart. If I've been too impetuous, too overbearing, I'm sorry—but I beg you to give me another chance."

To his surprise, she stroked his bristly cheek. As always, her touch quietened the tempest in his head. "Does this truly mean so much to you?"

"What the devil else do you think?" His grip tightened. What did his pride matter when his whole life hung in the balance? "I've never begged for anything. But I'm begging you to give me another chance. Don't you see we could build something grand between us?"

"Oh, yes." Her smile was melancholy, but her touch remained tender.

He leaned his cheek into her hand, starving for more sweet contact. "Then?"

To his regret, she withdrew her hand. If ever he'd doubted her power over him, he just needed to recall how her briefest touch soothed his demons. For one instant, he wondered if he'd be wiser to let her go. But immediately the thought of losing her made his gut cramp with denial. Whatever her ability to devastate his feelings, over the last days, she'd become essential to him.

"I ask your indulgence."

He caught her hand and lifted it for a kiss. "Anything."

"You might be sorry you said that."

"Just don't tell me you never want to see me again."

Her lips twitched. "It's not quite that bad."

That one small word "quite" struck like a knife. "How bad is it?"

His foreboding deepened when she withdrew her hand. "I'm going to leave you."

Those words beat such a death knell that it took him a few bleak moments to realize she was still talking. "I'll return to London on my own. I need time to think, and I can't think when I'm with you."

He needed a few more seconds to understand that she wasn't closing the door between them forever. "When can I see you again?"

The shake of her head expressed exasperation rather than denial, thank God. "Here's where I need you to cooperate. I ask you to leave me alone until I've questioned my heart and worked out what I want." Her helpless gesture sliced at him. "I can't expect you to understand. I hardly understand, myself. But you've thrown me completely off course. I'd intended to live alone and devote myself to Brandon. I had no plans to remarry."

"And you're still grieving for Henry."

She nodded. "Love doesn't let you go easily. Not real love."

He had a grim inkling that he was about to discover that for himself.

"So you want me to sit patiently and do nowt until you decide for or against me?" He sounded churlish, but he couldn't help it.

Her glance was amused but fond. "Perhaps patience is asking too much. But yes. With the rest of our lives at stake, you can grant me a couple of weeks to reflect on my decision and come to terms with what has passed."

"And if I won't agree?" Although what choice did he have?

Her jaw set in the stubborn line he'd first seen when she'd insisted upon joining a stranger on a frantic chase. "I'll know I can entrust neither myself nor my son to your care."

He scowled. "That's harsh."

"I know you're used to being in charge. After five years, so am I. Think of this as a test."

"How long must I wait?" he asked, still disgruntled. Now he'd tasted her, he didn't want her miles away, weighing his good and bad qualities. Especially as he had a horrid feeling that he was no competition for her beloved Henry.

Her eyes sharpened, reminding him yet again that her fragility was deceptive. "You don't have to agree."

"If I don't, you'll walk away without a backward glance."

"Never so coldhearted as that, but you've heard my proposal."

"And you've heard mine—if you decide in my favor, we're getting married."

She looked startled, although why she should, he

had no idea. After all, he could make ultimatums, too. "Now who's being uncompromising?"

He smiled. "The future promises to be interesting, doesn't it? It won't be a quiet life."

"So you agree?"

"Aye. When I have to, I can take the long way to my destination. I just wish I believed you felt a similar commitment."

She made a conciliatory gesture. "Everything has happened so fast. I haven't stood on solid ground since you stormed into my house and bullied the servants. I have to be sure."

Compassion flooded him, stronger than resentment. "Fenella, you can't be sure. Not completely. You just have to trust that your heart and your good sense lead you right. I know losing Henry shattered your world, and you're terrified that might happen again. But you can't spend your life afraid to take the next step."

"I still need to think."

"Don't think yourself back into isolation."

Displeasure darkened her eyes. "I asked you not to badger me."

A mixture of frustration and affection flattened his lips. "No, the wooing can wait until you make up your mind—which strikes me as a blasted widdershins way to go about things."

"Good." She paused. "Thank you."

"What about Brand? He's welcome to stay at the Beeches."

She frowned. "That rather defeats my purposes."

"Well, you could say you'll marry me, and we'll sort out our problems as we go. All four of us will make a home at the Beeches."

"Oh, Lord..." She raised a hand to her throat as though holding in her consent.

The flash of longing in her eyes took him back to the night's fiery intimacies. He realized that despite her fear, despite her loyalty to her dead husband, she was powerfully tempted.

He'd imagined himself powerless in this war between Fenella's past and a future that she'd never wished for. But he just might have a few weapons of his own.

Recognizing that, he was at last willing to step back. "I'll bring the boys up to London next week. Carey will enjoy seeing the sights. I'll take Brand around, too, then return him to you before we go home. Good enough?"

She looked doubtful. "Can you manage two eleven-year-old boys?"

He pretended to be insulted. "Madam, I'll have you know I captained a crew of Lascars as likely to cut your throat as give you good day—and bent them to my will. In comparison, Brandon and Carey will be a picnic."

Her laugh was rusty and carried the weight of her earlier tears. But he was glad to see her looking happier. He didn't want her carrying away the memory of a dour, difficult conversation—and a dour, difficult suitor.

"If Brand becomes unruly, send him home."

He took her hand again. She was leaving any moment, damn it. "If you need to reach me, send to the Beeches. Otherwise I'll be at the Townsend offices."

She regarded him with such wistfulness that he slung an arm around her and drew her down to rest her head on his shoulder. "It will all work out, Fenella."

"You must think I'm a dreadful witch, making all these conditions," she said in a muffled voice.

His hold tightened. She was worth a few sacrifices. He'd wait, and he'd do it without pestering her, even if it killed him. Which given the imperious, willful, impatient fellow he was, it was very likely to do. "I feel like a prince in a fairytale, set a series of impossible challenges to win the princess."

She smiled up at him. "You're a romantic, Anthony Townsend. Who knew?"

"You've made me one."

She didn't answer, but he supposed the way she pressed closer was response enough. As the light in the room strengthened to full day, they sat together in that undemanding embrace. And gradually a little of the peace he'd found in her arms last night returned to ease his soul.

When at last she raised her golden head and straightened, he itched to bring her back to him. But he'd made a promise, however much it pricked. Already.

Soon it would become purest hell. He never let other people set the agenda.

"I'd like to be on the way before the inn is busy and there's a chance someone might recognize me," she said.

He nodded, a hollow feeling in his gut like he let her go forever, which was absurd. But having found her, his deepest instinct was to keep her near. "Do you want breakfast?"

She shook her head. "No, I'll be in London in a little over an hour. I'll eat there. Please…let me go before I do something foolish."

He bit back a plea for her to stay and be as foolish as she liked. "I'll ring for the carriage."

The quiet scattered into the bustle of dressing, making travel arrangements, giving orders to servants, and Fenella tidying herself in the mirror. Despite Anthony's anguish, it was a joy to watch her perform such intimate and prosaic acts. He yearned for this serene daily life to start, with a lovely woman he cared for and respected. He thirsted to see her grow round with his child. He wanted the years ahead with her at his side.

Yet this perfect future hinged on something as unpredictable as a woman's will. His hopes seemed dangerously frail.

Within what felt like an instant, it was time for

Fenella to leave. And because he'd go through purgatory without her, even after only a few days, and because he had so few advantages in this battle against unseen forces, he caught her arm before she left. "I know you're going to think about Brandon and Henry, and what can go wrong, and how you cast your bonnet over a windmill, and you're not a lass to go chasing foolish whims and reckless dreams—"

"Anthony—"

Still the words poured from his lips, urgent, ardent, insistent. "But when you're alone at night in your big empty bed, and your sensible self insists that marrying a stranger is all too absurd, and really you suffered a moment's madness, but now you're all safe and back to reality again, I want you to remember this."

Without giving her a chance to protest, he bundled her up against him and sent his mouth crashing down into hers. He offered no gentle preliminaries, no coaxing persuasion. Instead he kissed her with all the fervent passion in his heart, a passion he hadn't come near to slaking last night, however sizzling those hours.

She stiffened, then abruptly curved into him as if she couldn't get enough of him. For a blissful interlude, everything was heat and need.

Until too soon, she pulled away. He fought the impulse to fling her onto the chaotic bed behind him and prove once and for all that they should stay together.

But beneath animal hunger lurked the vestiges of an honorable man, and he'd promised her time. So with agonized reluctance, he released her.

As she backed away, she stumbled. He caught her elbow to save her from falling. She was trembling. "Don't make me wait too long, Fenella."

Sucking in a shaky breath, she shook her head. Then to his surprise she touched his cheek in farewell and gave him a dazzling smile that set his heart somersaulting. "Your last card was an ace, my dear."

Before he could react to that astounding statement, she was gone.

CHAPTER THIRTEEN

"Fen, I saw Brandon on Monday. He was with Anthony Townsend," Caroline, Lady Beaumont said from her seat near the fire. "You didn't tell us he was in Town."

"Anthony? I mean, Mr. Townsend," Fenella stammered, color stinging her cheeks. She avoided the lovely brunette's questioning stare by pretending vast and unlikely interest in a plate of cucumber sandwiches. The three dashing widows met for afternoon tea in Helena, Countess of Crewe's luxurious drawing room in Berkeley Square.

"No," Caro said on a rising note. "Not...*Anthony.* Brandon. Shouldn't he be in school?"

"Um," Fenella said from beside the tea tray, completely caught out. She'd kept the events of those overwhelming days over a week ago to herself. She was so muddled and troubled that putting her tumultuous emotions into words was completely beyond her. Miraculously in her gossip-ridden world, news of her midnight flight from London hadn't spread. She thanked her loyal staff for that.

Helena turned from staring out into the rain. Tall, slender and black-haired, she was the pattern of elegance in her bronze afternoon gown. *"Anthony?"*

Fenella squirmed. Helena's curiosity was as sharp as a surgeon's scalpel. "I didn't know you were acquainted with Mr. Townsend, Caro."

Caro's dark blue eyes were alight with unholy interest. "When apparently you two are on first name terms."

"I... Brand's friends with Mr. Townsend's nephew."

"That must be the other boy I saw. They were playing cricket in Hyde Park," Caro said.

Despite herself, Fenella smiled. Whatever else resulted from their adventure, it seemed Anthony had worked out how he and his orphaned charge would deal together.

"Do you know Anthony Townsend, Helena?" Caro asked.

Helena's gimlet dark gaze didn't waver from Fenella. "No, but I've got a feeling I will before too much longer."

"He's frightfully clever and rich as Croesus. Silas and he do business together, so he came to dinner last summer. Interesting man, terrifyingly dynamic, and built like a battleship. But something of a rough diamond, I'd have said. All owts and nowts and thees and thous. I had to check to see he wasn't wearing hobnail boots."

"That's not fair," Fenella said hotly. "Rather you should admire a man who's made his way with such spectacular success purely on his own merits."

"Should she indeed?" Helena said archly, as Fenella realized that like a fool she'd played straight into Caro's game.

"She…she should," Fenella said, struggling to escape confiding what had happened between her and Anthony. She'd lay no money on her success. Now Caro and Hel scented scandal, they wouldn't leave her alone this side of Christmas. She'd been an idiot not to realize how closely her world rubbed shoulders with his.

With a laugh, Caro set down her cup. "Oh, give up, Fen. You're the world's worst liar. It's one of your greatest charms. You've been acting jumpy as a cat on a stove for days. I worried that you were coming down with something. You've been looking quite bilious."

"Bilious," Fenella said flatly.

"Yes," Helena said. "It's put us off our petits fours."

"Whereas instead you've come down with a case of the mysterious and wildly attractive Mr. Townsend," Caro said. "So stop torturing us and tell all."

Distressed, Fenella regarded her two fellow dashing widows.

For days, she'd hardly slept, and when she had, she'd

suffered dark and tormenting dreams where Henry became Anthony, and Anthony became Henry. Just this morning, she'd stirred before dawn to realize with horror that she couldn't picture Henry's face. Sobbing, she'd fumbled to light a candle, then grabbed his miniature that she kept beside her bed. She decided this couldn't go on. She wanted her peace back. However lonely. However dull. She'd begged Henry's forgiveness and decided to write to Anthony, refusing his proposal.

But now, hearing Anthony's name spoken spiked an invincible tide of longing. The thought of never seeing him again was unbearable.

She felt nauseous with indecision. No wonder Caro had remarked on her sickly appearance.

"Fen?" This time Helena's voice wasn't sly with knowledge, but edged with sincere concern. "Are you all right?"

"I..." she began, intending to lie her way out of this, no matter how ineptly. Then the worried affection in her friends' eyes defeated her shabby attempts at bravado. "No. No, I'm not all right."

Then to her utter mortification, she burst into tears.

"Oh, Fen, I'm so sorry," Caro wailed, rushing over to sit beside her and put her arm around her. "I'm a great blundering fool. It's none of my business. I shouldn't have asked. If that brute has hurt you, I'll set the dogs on him."

"You don't have any dogs," Fenella blubbered through the hands she'd placed over her streaming eyes. "And he's not a brute. In fact, he's…he's rather wonderful."

"Is he?" Helena asked drily, approaching to pass her a handkerchief.

"Yes, yes, he is," Fenella said, gratefully seizing the lacy square and blowing her nose. "Oh, this is just stupid. I don't know what's wrong with me."

She raised her head in time to catch a meaningful glance between her friends.

"Don't you?" Helena asked.

"Tell us everything. You'll feel better if you do," Caro said.

"I doubt it," Fenella said, blowing her nose again.

"Try," Helena said.

"You surely can't feel much worse," Caro said. "And you know we're dying of curiosity."

"Caro," Helena said reprovingly.

Her lovely friend shrugged her slender shoulders. "Well, we'll feel better if she talks, even if Fen doesn't."

Despite her wretchedness, Fenella gave a broken laugh. "You make my need for a little privacy sound positively selfish."

"Keeping everything to yourself obviously doesn't make you happy," Helena said.

Fenella twisted the damp handkerchief between her shaking hands. "I thought you were on my side."

"As always, I'm on the side of scientific truth," Helena said loftily.

Somehow that remark had Fenella pouring out the

whole story, only faltering into silence when she and Anthony arrived at the Rainbow and Angel.

"Then he said..." That discomfiting blush rose again. "Well, you can see why I'm in a complete mess."

"Not fair, Fen," Caroline protested. "You can't stop there."

Helena cast Caro a repressive look. "Leave the poor woman a scrap of dignity, you dreadful creature. We can imagine what happened." Then spoiled her defense by asking, "So did you enjoy it?"

To her surprise, Fenella answered with complete honesty. "It was earth-shattering."

"Good Lord," Helena murmured, looking gratifyingly envious. "Aren't you lucky?"

Caro didn't say anything, but Fenella glimpsed a faint knowing smile. For the last six months, Caro and Helena's brother Silas, Lord Stone, had conducted a discreet affair. Undoubtedly she was familiar with how passion could turn the act of love into a transcendent experience.

"Then he asked me to marry him…"

"Hold on. He proposed after only two days?" Helena said in shock. "He must have fallen in love at first sight. How romantic."

"I told you—when we met, he wanted to strangle me. And love has nothing to do with this."

"Don't be a fool, Fen," Caro said. "You're head over heels, and by the sound of it, so is Mr. Townsend."

Aghast, Fenella stared at her. "You're wrong. I've

been in love. It wasn't like this. It was bright and kind and joyful—and easy."

"Fen, I'm no expert on love. After all, I imagined I was in love with that toad Crewe," Helena said, making rare reference to her late, unlamented husband. "But I'm fairly sure it comes in many guises. You won't love Anthony Townsend the same way you loved Henry."

"*Love* Henry," Fenella said sharply, shying away from the guilt and betrayal infesting her soul since she'd succumbed to sin and bedded Anthony.

Caro observed her with a compassionate understanding, new since she'd fallen in love with Silas. "That's what's behind your unhappiness, isn't it?"

Fenella's fists closed on her knees. "How can I love someone else when I still love Henry? How can I be so fickle that my heart changed within two days?"

"What did you say?" Helena asked.

"What?" Fenella asked, frowning.

"What did you say when Mr. Townsend asked you to marry him?" Helena said patiently.

"I told him to leave me alone while I think about it," she said in dejection.

"While you come up with reasons to say no, you mean." Caro caught Fenella's hand and spoke with heartfelt urgency. "Listen to me, Fenella Deerham, and listen well. There's something I need to say."

Fenella snatched her hand away and regarded her friend almost with dislike. "Your advice isn't reliable.

You're in love. Of course you want me to dive in headfirst."

Caro's mouth turned down, and briefly she looked like the dissatisfied, unhappy woman Fenella had first met two years ago. "Nobody knows better than you that life is unfair and joy can be fleeting. You've been offered a chance for new happiness. I hate to think fear is stopping you from taking it."

"I don't know why you're in Mr. Townsend's corner," Fenella said sourly. "You hardly know him."

"If he got you into bed, he's obviously a remarkable man. You've had London on its knees since Hel and I dragged you back into society, kicking and screaming and saying you didn't want to play. And you haven't cared a whit for the admiration. Men fall at your feet, and all you do is smile coolly and go on your merry way, safely locked away from life. If Anthony Townsend has made you cry your eyes out, he's special."

"That's unfair," Fenella said, nettled. "You make me sound so cold."

"Not cold, unaware."

She surged to her feet and stared furiously down at Caro. "You're a great one to talk about taking chances on love. You love Silas with all your heart, yet you won't marry him. He wants more from you than a hole in the corner liaison—he deserves more. But you won't see past your miserable marriage to know you've got a good man and you're doing him a vile injustice."

Caro paled under her attack. "Silas and I have an understanding."

"No, you haven't. But he's so much in love, he's willing to take what you'll give him, rather than nothing. You're starving him to death, and the worst part is you can't see it. You, Caroline Beaumont, are in no position to lecture me about being brave."

"Fen..." Helena said warningly.

Parker, Helena's butler, cleared his throat in the doorway. "Lord Stone has called, my lady."

An energetic, long-limbed man with untidy tawny hair strode into the room. Raindrops glittered on his shoulders, proof the weather hadn't improved. "For God's sake, Parker, this is my house, even if I don't damn well live here. There's no need to announce me."

"My dear brother, polite as ever, I see," Helena said, as Parker left after a bow that expressed long-suffering tolerance.

"Good evening, sis." Silas kissed Helena on the cheek, then glanced across the room. "Good evening, Fenella. Caro, we're engaged for the theatre tonight, or had you forgotten? I've been cooling my heels in Grosvenor Square waiting for you to come home, and eventually thought I'd better come looking for you. I should have known you'd still be gossiping with the coven."

With a shock, Fenella realized that afternoon had flowed into night. As if to confirm that, the ormolu clock on the mantel chimed seven. The cloudy day meant Helena had ordered candles when her guests arrived.

"Polite and charming," Caro said, but rose to kiss Silas on the lips. In public, the couple behaved—mostly—within the bounds of propriety. But here with family and close friends, they made no secret of their liaison.

"Of course, Fenella isn't a witch." He smiled down at her, then the laughter left his voice. "Fen, you've been crying. I'm sorry. I shouldn't have barged in."

She shook her head and spoke through agonizing embarrassment. Could this day get any more humiliating? "No, I'm glad you're here. Caro and I were about to come to blows."

"A dashed useful umpire, that's me," he said, but his touch was gentle when he kissed her cheek and drew her down to sit beside him.

"Would you like tea?" Helena asked, turning to the tray. "I can ask for some more."

Silas looked disgusted. "Tea, at this hour? You'll get me thrown out of my clubs."

"Brandy, then?"

His eyes met Caro's, and the silent communication between them pierced Fenella with longing. She and Anthony had shared a similar bond. Or at least started to.

Silas didn't mention the theatre again, but relaxed on the sofa, stretching out his long legs in their black trousers. "A small one. I haven't dined yet."

Fenella expected he and Caro had romantic plans for an intimate meal after the play, then a night of making love. She shifted subtly on the chair as she recalled Anthony's big, virile body pounding into her. Since leaving him, she hadn't only suffered emotionally. That night at the Rainbow and Angel had reminded her how much she'd missed the physical side of marriage.

"So are you going to tell me why you could cut the atmosphere with a knife when I came in?" Silas asked with deceptive laziness.

"What do you know about Anthony Townsend?" Helena asked.

"Helena, for pity's sake!" Fenella snapped.

Silas's disconcertingly intelligent hazel eyes settled on her. "Ah."

Fenella's cheeks burned again. Silas's ahs could speak volumes. "Brandon is great friends with his nephew."

"His brother's son? That was a horrible tragedy when William and his wife were lost at sea. The lad's lucky to have a steadfast fellow like Townsend to turn to."

"So you like him?" Caro asked.

"Yes, I do. Very much. Capable chap. More than capable. Brilliant. Came in to rescue the government from fiscal disaster last year. Word is there's a peerage in the offing from a grateful nation."

Caro sent Fenella a significant look before she

returned to quizzing Silas. "But what about his character? Would you trust him?"

Silas's expressive brows rose. "What's all this sudden interest in Anthony Townsend? Are you planning to throw me over for a richer prize, my love?"

"He probably doesn't tease," Caro retorted.

"Yes, he does," Fenella said, then wanted to kick herself.

Silas studied her like one of the botanical specimens in his greenhouse. "He's a fine man. I can't think of a better. Even if his manners aren't the most polished."

This time, Fenella restrained her response.

After a thoughtful pause, Silas said softly, "But I doubt whether my liking has any bearing on the matter. The question is whether Fenella likes him."

"If you were any sharper, Silas Nash, you'd cut yourself," she muttered.

He laughed and picked up her hand to place a casual kiss on her knuckles. "There I have my answer."

"Silas, I had an interesting chat about you the other day," Helena said, offering Fenella a reprieve. Now that attention focused on someone else, Fenella dragged in a relieved breath.

"Oh?" Silas said, accepting a crystal glass from his sister and raising it to his lips. "What the devil mischief have I been up to now?"

Helena didn't smile, but ranged herself in front of the fire with a curiously belligerent stance. "The pertinent issue is what you haven't been up to—or what you won't get up to, rather."

"I'm all ears," he said idly. Caro shifted to stand behind the sofa and rest her hand on his shoulder. Fenella had long noticed that the two lovers could hardly bear to be in the same room without touching. They'd come together at the end of last season, so few people knew about their affair. But she couldn't imagine the secret surviving once the annual round of balls and parties began in the spring. "Who's been spreading wicked tales?"

"I ran into Mr. Browning at Kew Gardens."

A resonant silence fell, the significance of which only Silas and Helena seemed to understand.

"Ah."

Fenella was close enough to feel his tension.

Helena's gaze sharpened on his face. "He said he'd invited you on the camellia collecting expedition to China next year, but you'd said no."

For once, there was no hint of humor in Silas's face. "London offers too much entertainment for me to forsake it at present."

"Really, Silas? That's hard to believe. Ever since you were a boy, you've talked about hunting new plants in the East and how you'd devote your life to exploration and discovery."

"Well, priorities change when one grows up," he said with unaccustomed brusqueness. "My colleagues at the Horticultural Society will have to manage without me while they grub around beside the Yellow River for pretty little flowers. I find this subject tedious in the extreme. Let's go back to interrogating Fenella about her new beau."

"No, please," Fenella said fervently.

"Silas, do you really want to go?" Caro moved around the sofa until she could see his face.

"I don't want to leave you, my darling." He smiled, but Fenella saw it was an effort. "It's no sacrifice to stay."

"But this is a once in a lifetime opportunity," Caro said urgently.

"It's a pity they don't take ladies on scientific expeditions," Fenella said.

Helena's lips curled in a sardonic smile as she continued to study her brother. "But this expedition is different. It's a diplomatic mission as much as a plant hunt. Mr. Browning is taking his wife. So are Sir Richard Bentley and Lord Parrish."

Caro brightened. "Silas, you know I've longed to travel. Perhaps we could…"

His expression closed, and he suddenly looked much older than the lighthearted man Fenella thought she knew. "I've said I won't go, Caro. If you like, I'll take you to Italy after Christmas. That will placate your yen for adventure."

Caro stared at him with dismay. "Ladies can go, but only if they're wives. You're not taking up this wonderful chance to see China because you can't take your mistress." She stopped, her mind clearly making connections. "Of course you can't. If it's officially sanctioned, you'd create an international scandal if you turned up with your doxy in tow."

Fenella's protesting "Caro" clashed with Silas's savage "You're not my doxy."

He leaped to his feet. "If you don't mind, this isn't a discussion I want to have before witnesses." He shot his sister a savage glare that made Fenella wince in sympathy. "Congratulations, Hel. You wanted to cause trouble and you've succeeded."

Helena remained stalwart under his blistering anger. "You know, Silas, if you and Caro married, you could be off to Peking tomorrow, and nobody would raise an eyebrow."

"Marriage isn't for us," he said in a stilted voice, although his eyes continued to threaten murder.

Helena clicked her tongue with disapproval. "For shame, to trifle with a lady's feelings and reputation."

"Helena…" he said on a growl of warning.

Caro straightened, her face drawn with misery. "It's my fault we're not married. You all know that. I swore I'd never take another husband."

Helena made an impatient noise. "Why on earth not? Freddie was undoubtedly a blockhead. So what? You and my brother are in love, and my brother isn't a blockhead—most of the time."

"Thank you, dear sister," he bit out.

She sighed. "Well, it's stupid. Just because Caro's a

coward, you're going to miss out on fulfilling a dream. Even more asinine, it's Caro's dream, too. She always said she wanted to see the world and break out of her old, stale, dull life. A trip to China does that in spades."

Silas extended his hand to Caro. "Come, my love. I'll take you home."

Caro didn't shift, and Fenella who knew her so well, read the battle going on inside her. It was a battle she understood much better since she'd met Anthony and discovered she, too, was trapped between the past and a beckoning, risky future.

"Helena's right, you know," Caro said slowly.

"Why would I want China when I have you?" Silas asked with a fair approximation of his usual good nature.

Caro squared her shoulders and looked directly at the man she loved. Her jaw was set in an obstinate line, and her hands clenched at her sides. But Fenella saw the terror shining in her eyes. "You could have both."

Her offer didn't noticeably cheer him up. He ran his hand through his hair and looked grimly at Caro. "I promised I wouldn't pressure you about marriage."

"I know." She paused, then spoke in a hurry. "But asking me to marry you after six blissful months doesn't count as pressure."

Silas took a couple of moments to examine what she said, then such naked joy filled his face that fresh tears sprang to Fenella's eyes. Not altogether with happiness for her friends. Caro's courage threw her own lack of daring into stark relief.

"Do you mean it, sweetheart?" he asked in a hoarse voice.

Caro's laugh cracked with emotion, but her reply rang with confidence. "Yes, I do."

Silas caught her hand and stared into her eyes. "Caroline Beaumont, the love of my life, would you do me the inestimable honor of becoming my wife?"

Caro's smile matched his in elation. She lifted one hand to touch his face with such tenderness that it set Fenella's lonely heart aching anew. "Seeing you asked so nicely, my beloved Lord Stone, I just have to say yes."

"Oh, my love," he said in a broken voice and hauled her into his arms for a fervent kiss that paid no heed to their audience.

"At last," Helena said, looking justifiably smug. "I'll ring for champagne."

CHAPTER FOURTEEN

*A*nthony devoted the morning to chopping wood behind the hay barn. He wasn't much use for anything else these days. There was nobody around to bother him—which suited him fine. In the past two weeks, the outdoor staff had taken to scattering toward the farthest corners of the estate to avoid their irascible master.

He couldn't say he blamed them.

Since Fenella had left, his mood had grown increasingly black. For the first few days, her parting words had convinced him she'd relent. He'd leaped on every mail delivery as if it offered a reprieve from a death sentence.

In London, he'd been as excited as an infatuated schoolboy at the thought of seeing his inamorata, but they hadn't encountered each other. Not even Brand's safe return to Curzon Street had provided a forbidden glimpse.

A hundred times, Anthony had been on the verge of ordering his carriage and setting out in pursuit of his elusive darling. After all, women liked to play games— perhaps Fenella tested his purpose by saying, "Don't touch me," when she really wanted him to lay siege to her.

But something always stopped him. Probably her austere expression when she'd asked for time.

Time! Such a little word to cause this agony of soul and body.

For a glorious, too brief interval, he'd held Fenella Deerham in his arms and the world had turned into heaven. The idea that she'd allow him no more left him wandering in darkness. The only thing that kept creeping despair at bay was mindless, vigorous phys- ical labor. Which was why he was outside on this freezing day, working like a navvy, instead of sitting back and giving orders like the aristocrat he'd never be, no matter how he tried.

The thought that his coarse manners might have repulsed fastidious, wellborn Fenella Deerham made him want to smash something. And as a result the house had firewood into the next decade.

He sank the ax into a block of wood, hearing that satisfying split, tugged it free, then raised his head from his furious activity. Someone drove a carriage at speed toward the yard on the other side of the stable block.

Swearing under his breath, he brushed the sweat from his face. What bloody idiot intruded on him, expecting a fair hearing? His temper heated as he shrugged on his shirt and marched around the stable to see who was brave enough to disturb his fit of self-pity.

His heart slammed to a stop. His hand opened, and the ax clattered to the cobblestones.

A stylish carriage bowled toward him at a cracking pace. Holding the reins with an aplomb that would take his breath away, if he had any breath left, was the woman he'd once called a useless ornament to society.

With a flourish Fenella drew the horses to a neat stop, making the high-stepping blacks arch their necks and stamp their hooves. Her bonnet had fallen back and dangled from two bright yellow ribbons. Her fine golden hair curled around her face in wild abandon that reminded him how she'd looked lying in his arms. A flush marked her cheeks and her eyes glittered.

A useless ornament? This woman could conquer worlds with a mere flick of her elegant fingers.

Those brilliant blue eyes found him. "Did you mean it?" she asked in a hard voice he'd never heard her use before.

With the question, hope lurched into vigorous life. Immediately deciphering her question, he grinned in delight as though he hadn't spent a fortnight eating his heart out over her. "Of course."

"Good." She flung the reins aside as he strode up to the carriage.

He seized her by the waist and lifted her to the ground. "Come with me."

"The horses?"

"Won't go far." With a careless toss, he hitched the reins over a convenient post. Frankly, he couldn't give a damn if the nags ended up in Scotland. He twined his arm around her and swept her into the noonday hush of the stables.

"Are you—" she began shakily.

"I am."

"Oh, Lord," she gasped on an excited laugh that whipped him to a frenzy.

In an empty stall, he slid her onto a fragrant pile of hay and came down over her, already tugging at the front fall of his breeches.

She stretched out on the makeshift bed and stripped her gloves off, flinging them into the shadows. In the half light, the certainty shining in her eyes made his blood rush.

"Speak now, or forever hold your peace," he said roughly.

Even burning like flame in his arms, she hadn't smiled like this. Like she knew every sensual secret. And meant to reveal those mysteries to him alone, lucky sap he was. "That sounds dauntingly matrimonial."

"Aye, it does."

"Then we're of one mind."

"I haven't had a mind since I met you," he muttered,

and at last kissed her. She responded with an abandon that, even without her words, told him she'd overcome all doubt. Distantly he was aware that she'd agreed to marry him, but right now he had other fish to fry.

His tongue delved deep into her mouth until she whimpered with anticipation. The knot in her bonnet ribbons defied his shaking hands. Swearing, he tore it apart. She made a sound, half-appalled, half-admiring, as she released the front fastenings of her green carriage dress. Clearly she didn't trust him not to rip that to shreds as well. Wise woman.

When the stylish jacket parted at last, his greedy hands rose to cover her lovely breasts. She wrenched her lips from his and fell back into the hay with a gurgle of laughter. "Don't wait."

With one ruthless movement he swept her skirts up, revealing lacy white drawers. "Nice," he grunted. Words longer than one syllable were beyond him.

"Rip them," she gasped. She made no secret that she craved this joining, and he loved it.

Laughing exultantly, he obeyed. Feverishly he stroked her thighs and cleft and stomach. But neither of them had the patience for lengthy preliminaries.

His chest heaving, he hooked his hands under her knees and plunged inside her. She was hot and ready and needy. They were both too desperate for finesse. Her swift, wild climax astonished him, then he was lost in the gathering storm.

Vaguely through his primitive drive to possess and

please and mark, he felt her reach another peak. Then fire blasted him, and on a long groan of release, he filled her with a titanic torrent of longing and loneliness and desire.

Utterly exhausted, breathlessly happy, he slumped over her. The remnants of her pleasure still quivered through her. Their passion had scoured the world clean.

As the fierce beat of his heart calmed and he returned to earth from the outer limits of the sky, he became aware of how tenderly she touched him. Little, glancing caresses across his hair, his ears, his neck, his bare shoulder where his shirt had slid down during that incendiary encounter. The erratic exploration made his heart clench with poignant emotion.

"I'm assuming you missed me," she murmured unsteadily, affectionate amusement running like a warm river under her teasing.

He leaned his forehead into her neck. The evocative scent of the stables surrounded him, but richer still was the scent of Fenella's satisfaction. "Like the very devil."

"I missed you, too."

"I guessed that when you galloped up like the hounds of hell pursued you. Did you come all the way from London like that?"

"A nervous groom accompanied me as far as Winchester. I left him to recover his breath at a tavern outside the city. I didn't want an audience when we met again."

Anthony smiled reminiscently and kissed her neck before rolling off her. "I must be crushing you."

"It's rather…exciting."

"Nowhere near as exciting as you flying in like a Valkyrie set on my seduction. For future reference, I find the sight of your delicate self controlling a team of huge, snorting beasts uncontrollably arousing."

"For future reference?" she asked drily, raising a hand to tug a wisp of straw from his hair.

He settled her on his chest. The hay provided a surprisingly comfortable couch. "Aye. A wife needs to know these things."

"So we're getting married, then," she said neutrally.

"We are indeed, lass. Soon."

Her expression softened. "I love the way you call me lass."

"That's a damned good thing, given you're likely to hear it for the next fifty years or so. Don't try and say no. I only accepted your bold invitation just now because you said you'd make an honest man of me afterward."

"A lady can't change her mind?"

"No."

"You're very highhanded."

He stared into her bright eyes. "I suspect you can handle me the way you handle that team of horses."

Her smile was smug. "You could be right."

"So we'll marry." He'd known the moment she blazed back into his life that she intended to stay, but it was satisfying to set out his agenda. "Although I'd very much like to know what tipped the balance in my favor."

She sat up and started to button her dress until he reached to stop her. "Memories of you as a wanton milkmaid will fuel my fantasies until I'm old and decrepit. Don't take the reality away yet."

Her lips, full and red after his kisses, twitched. "You know, now that I'm staying, we can take a tumble in the stables whenever you feel the urge."

Without shifting his gaze from her, he lay full length on the hay and crossed his arms behind his head. Her gaping bodice gave him tantalizing glimpses of her breasts. Arousal stirred lazily, but he reined it in. This capitulation was too new and hard-won to take for granted.

"What a glorious prospect. Now put me out of my misery and tell me why you came back."

The hungry inspection she devoted to his body made him wonder why in Hades he wasted time on talk when they had a whole stable to themselves and an afternoon to enjoy it. "You don't look too miserable."

"You should have seen me half an hour ago."

He'd spoken lightly, but she must have heard an echo of his earlier desolation. Remorse deepened her eyes to sapphire, and she leaned down to kiss him. "I'm sorry. I was utterly wretched without you, too."

"I've been as cranky as a bear. Ask Carey."

She started and glanced around nervously. "Oh, good heavens, I didn't even think of him. Where is he?"

Anthony sat up and caught her hand. "He's doing Latin translation at the vicarage. It gives you some idea of how impossible I've been that every morning, he positively gallops away to his studies."

She laughed. "Oh, dear. That bad?"

He kissed her slender fingers. "Tell me, Fenella."

The amusement drained from her face. "That morning in Croydon, you called me a coward. So did my closest friends when they heard what had happened. Yesterday I saw one of those dear friends find the courage to step beyond her past and into a new future. I realized then that over the years, my grief for Henry had become a cage." She shook her tumbled hair back from her face. "I don't want to live in a cage anymore, Anthony. I want to live in the open with you."

He was so moved by her confession that he needed to clear his throat before he spoke. "Fenella, will you do something for me?"

"Anything."

Her quick response made him smile. "Now that sounds right wifely, lass." His voice turned somber. "Will you tell me about Henry?"

Fenella snatched her hand free and stared at him in shock. The voluptuous languor lingering from that heated bout in the hay trickled away to leave a chill on her skin. "About Henry? Why? Surely you're not jealous of a dead man."

Anthony's gaze didn't waver as he shook his dark head. "That's not why I'm asking. Although you need to know that I have been jealous of him. Unforgivably so. Because he has your steadfast love." His spoke in that deep velvet bass that always made her shiver with feminine awareness. "But I'm not jealous of him anymore. Today I reckon I no longer need to be."

After rolling around under Anthony in the full light of day—in a stable, no less—she shouldn't be able to muster a blush. But her cheeks stung none-theless. Her eyelashes flickered down, and she pretended interest in dusting off her dark green merino skirts.

"If you no longer consider him a…rival, why do you want to know about him?"

He shrugged. "For many reasons. Because he was dear to you, and I care about what you care about. Because he's Brandon's father." He spoke slowly and very deliberately, as though he picked his way through a jungle of words to find precisely the right ones. "And because I believe you need to make some ritual act to let him go. We owe homage to his ghost. Only once we pay that homage can you turn your face to a life with me."

The breath jammed in her throat. What staggering generosity of spirit. Every time she thought she understood Anthony Townsend, he revealed some new and marvelous aspect of his character.

Still, she balked at praising an old lover to the skies when she'd just surrendered to a new one. "For heaven's sake, I just let you tumble me in a haystack. I couldn't be more committed."

"Indulge me, my darling." He cupped her jaw and kissed her with a thoroughness that made her toes curl. "I don't want any shadows hanging over us."

The unfamiliar, unexpected endearment bolstered her courage. "He'll always be part of my life."

Anthony's smile was irresistibly sweet. He held his arm out. "Come here. You're too far away."

She accepted the invitation without hesitation. Once she was curled into his side, she murmured, "You mightn't like what you hear."

Anthony's laugh was a comforting rumble. "What? Because he was a good man? You misjudge me. I'd never wish you unhappy—and I'm grateful that you had someone worthy of you."

She tilted her head back to meet his intense dark stare. "When it comes to good men, I've been lucky twice over."

He kissed her gently. "I'll do my best, lass. I swear that on my life."

The kiss vanquished her misgivings. But because talking at length about Henry hurt, even five years after his death, she faltered at the beginning. "It's an ordinary story. Our fathers were best friends at

Eton. Henry and I knew each other from babyhood."

Anthony settled her more comfortably against him, so she felt safe and cherished in a way she hadn't since she'd received the devastating news from Waterloo. "A bit like Carey and Brand."

The reminder of her beloved son made continuing easier. "Yes, like that. You could say the match was arranged, but by the time we wed, we were so mad for each other, that wasn't important. Henry was all I'd ever wanted."

"Handsome?"

She dissected the question for any resentment, but all she heard was friendly curiosity. "As an angel. Especially in his regimentals. But his looks weren't what made him so special. He was by nature a contented man. I think that was his greatest gift—happiness." She pressed her cheek to Anthony's heart, finding strength in its steady beat. "I'm not explaining this very well."

He shaped one hand to her jaw and cradled her face against his chest. "You're doing fine."

Uncanny how his strength flowed into her. "But Henry was a soldier and England was at war. In our eight years, we rarely had more than a few months together at a time. I'd worked up the nerve to follow the drum with him in Spain when I fell pregnant."

How long it was since she'd thought of Henry in his prime. His early, heroic death had tainted every happy memory. Which suddenly struck her as a pity. And vilely unjust to a man who deserved to be remembered with a smile.

"So you spent most of your life missing him?"

She wasn't surprised Anthony understood. "Yes. Although there's a difference between knowing someone can come home and knowing you'll never see them again. And he was tired of war well before Waterloo. When we thought Boney was finished in 1814, Henry was so looking forward to coming home to Brand and me. And more children. We would both have loved that." Her voice broke, and she blinked away tears.

His arm tightened. "Do you want to stop?"

"Do you want to hear more?"

"Aye. But not if it's too difficult."

Fenella pressed closer. His protective warmth had lured her from the first, even when he'd been shouting at her. "It's easier to tell you than I thought it would be."

"You describe a paragon."

She smiled wistfully. "I'm sure I've idealized him. Of course he had his faults. A tendency to accept a superficial impression as fact. Impetuosity. And he was nowhere near as clever as you are. But that didn't spoil the man he was. He brought sunshine wherever he went."

"And you feel like you've lived in night ever since."

"Yes."

"I'm sorry you lost him, Fenella."

"So am I." Then she surprised herself by saying,

"He'd have liked you. Despite your apparent differences, both of you have…integrity. It's a rare and precious quality."

"Thank you." His lips brushed the top of her head. "I think I'd have liked him, too, although I'd envy him his pretty wife. He sounds like an exceptional man. I can see why you've clung to his memory all these years."

Fenella made herself sit up and meet Anthony's eyes. She didn't underestimate how hard it must be for him to hear her loving recollections of another man. Yet he did this for her—so that she could join him in a new life. "I thought I'd grieve forever."

"And that's no longer the case?" he asked slowly.

"I'll always miss Henry and regret his loss. But I've changed out of all recognition since the night this big brute of a man stormed into my parlor and shook me from my torpor."

Anthony smiled at her as if she was a miracle of creation. "You know I love you, don't you?"

At the quiet declaration, her heart stuttered into stillness. Then it began to beat deliberate and hard, like a military drum marking a slow march. She took Anthony's powerful hand in hers and stared into that roughhewn, fascinating face. She saw intelligence and strength and kindness.

And, yes, love.

"I hoped."

"And can you imagine ever loving me?"

She gave a huff of amusement, although she knew

what it had cost him to ask the question. "Don't be a nitwit, Anthony. Of course I love you. It took me completely by surprise because it's not at all like what I felt for Henry. Our love was like a beautiful clear lake, unruffled and calm. When I'm with you, I feel like I'm aboard a great ship on a storm-tossed ocean. It's exciting and daring and reassuring, all at the same time. And I feel like I'm heading for somewhere wonderful and exotic."

"Oh, my darling," he murmured and kissed her softly on the lips. "I don't deserve you."

She pulled away and regarded him sternly. "Of course you do. I was blessed to find love in my first marriage, and I've been doubly blessed to find it in my second." Her voice roughened. "And I feel Henry would approve. He was never a jealous, covetous man."

Anthony kissed her again and rose to his feet, extending his hand to help her up. "I know two people who will definitely approve."

"The boys?" She laughed with almost unbearable gladness. "Oh, yes. They'll vote for anything to save them from going back to Eton. To think, we'll all live here as a family on your beautiful estate."

He raised her hand to his lips. "We have a lifetime of love ahead, my darling."

She stepped into the shelter of his powerful body. The cold, lonely days were over at last. She was in love with Anthony Townsend, and the world glowed warm and full of light. "I can hardly wait."

ABOUT THE AUTHOR

ANNA CAMPBELL has written 10 multi award-winning historical romances for Grand Central Publishing and Avon HarperCollins, and her work is published in 22 languages. She has also written 21 bestselling independently published romances, including her series, The Dashing Widows and The Lairds Most Likely. Anna has won numerous awards for her Regency-set stories including Romantic Times Reviewers Choice, the Booksellers Best, the Golden Quill (three times), the Heart of Excellence (twice), the Write Touch, the Aspen Gold (twice) and the Australian Romance Readers Association's favorite historical romance (five times). Her books have three times been nominated for Romance Writers of America's prestigious RITA Award, and three times for Australia's Romantic Book of the Year. When she's not traveling the world seeking inspiration for her stories, Anna lives on the beautiful east coast of Australia.

Anna loves to hear from her readers. You can find her at:

Website: www.annacampbell.com

facebook.com/AnnaCampbellFans

twitter.com/AnnaCampbellOz

bookbub.com/authors/anna-campbell

goodreads.com/AnnaCampbell

ALSO BY ANNA CAMPBELL

Claiming the Courtesan

Untouched

Tempt the Devil

Captive of Sin

My Reckless Surrender

Midnight's Wild Passion

The Sons of Sin series:

Seven Nights in a Rogue's Bed

Days of Rakes and Roses

A Rake's Midnight Kiss

What a Duke Dares

A Scoundrel by Moonlight

Three Proposals and a Scandal

The Dashing Widows:

The Seduction of Lord Stone

Tempting Mr. Townsend

Winning Lord West

Pursuing Lord Pascal

Charming Sir Charles

Catching Captain Nash

Lord Garson's Bride

The Lairds Most Likely:

The Laird's Willful Lass

The Laird's Christmas Kiss

The Highlander's Lost Lady

Christmas Stories:

The Winter Wife

Her Christmas Earl

A Pirate for Christmas

Mistletoe and the Major

A Match Made in Mistletoe

The Christmas Stranger

Other Books:

These Haunted Hearts

Stranded with the Scottish Earl

THE SEDUCTION OF LORD STONE

(The Dashing Widows Book 1)

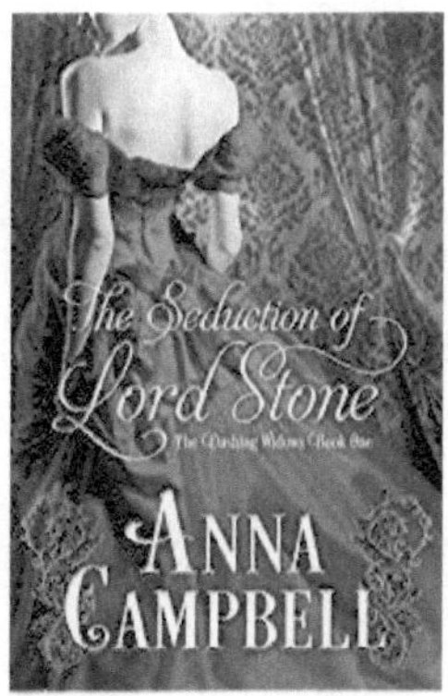

For this reckless widow, love is the most dangerous game of all.

Caroline, Lady Beaumont, arrives in London seeking excitement after ten dreary years of marriage and an even drearier year of mourning. That means conquering society, dancing like there's no tomorrow, and taking a lover to provide passion without promises. Promises, in this dashing widow's dictionary, equal prison. So what is an adventurous lady to do when she loses her heart to a notorious rake who, for the first time in his life, wants forever?

Devilish Silas Nash, Viscount Stone is in love at last with a beautiful, headstrong widow bent on playing the field. Worse, she's enlisted his help to set her up with his disreputable best friend. No red-blooded man takes such a challenge lying down, and Silas schemes to seduce his darling into his arms, warm, willing and besotted. But will his passionate plots come undone against a woman determined to act the mistress, but never the wife?

Now Helena is free, and this time, come hell or high water, West won't let her escape him again.

His weapon of choice is seduction, and in this particular game, he's an acknowledged master. Now that he and Helena are under one roof at the year's most glamorous house party, he intends to counter her every argument with breathtaking pleasure. Could it be that Lady Crewe's dashing days are numbered?

All that glitters...

Gervaise Dacre, Lord Pascal needs to marry money to save his estate, devastated after a violent storm. He's never much liked his reputation as London's handsomest man, but it certainly comes in handy when the time arrives to seek a rich bride. Unfortunately, the current crop of debutantes bores him silly, and he finds himself praying for a sensible woman with a generous dowry.

When he meets Dashing Widow Amy Mowbray, it seems all his prayers have been answered. Until he finds himself in thrall to the lovely widow, and his mercenary quest becomes dangerously complicated. Soon he's much more interested in passion than in pounds, shillings and pence. What happens if Amy discovers the sordid truth behind his whirlwind courtship? And if she does, will she see beyond his original, selfish motives to the ardent love that lies unspoken in his sinful heart?

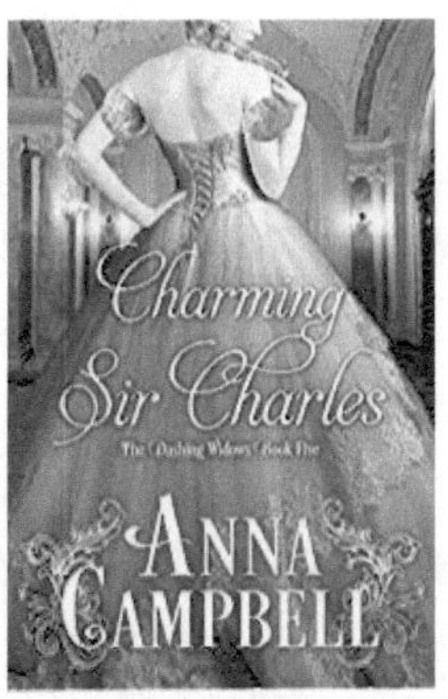

Matchmaking mayhem in Mayfair!

Sally Cowan, Countess of Norwood, spent ten miserable years married to an overbearing oaf. Now she's free, she plans to have some fun. But before she kicks her heels up, this Dashing Widow sets out to launch her pretty, headstrong niece Meg into society and find her a good husband.

When rich and charming Sir Charles Kinglake gives every sign that he can't get enough of Meg's company, Sally is delighted to play chaperone at all their meetings. Charles is everything that's desirable in a gentleman suitor. How disastrous, when over the course of the season's most elegant house party, Sally realizes that desire is precisely the name of the game. She's found her niece's perfect match—but she wants him for herself!

There are none so blind as those who will not see...

From the moment Sir Charles Kinglake meets sparkling Lady Norwood, he's smitten. He courts her as a gentleman should—dancing with her at every glittering ball, taking her to the theatre, escorting her around London. Because she's acting as chaperone to her niece, that means most times, Meg accompanies them. The lack of privacy chafes a man consumed by desire, but Charles's intentions are honorable, and he's willing to work within the rules to win the wife he wants.

However when he discovers that his careful pursuit has convinced Sally he's interested in Meg rather than her, he flings the rules out the window. When love is at stake, who cares about a little scandal? It's time for charming Sir Charles to abandon the subtle approach and play the passionate lover, not the society suitor!

Now with everything at sixes and sevens, Sir Charles risks everything to show lovely Lady Norwood they make the perfect pair!

CATCHING CAPTAIN NASH

(The Dashing Widows Book 6)

Home is the sailor, home from the sea...

Five years after he's lost off the coast of South America, presumed dead, Captain Robert Nash escapes cruel captivity, and returns to London and the bride he loves, but barely knows. When he stumbles back into the family home, he's appalled to find himself gate-crashing the party celebrating his wife's engagement to another man.

This gallant naval officer is ready to take on any challenge; but five years is a long time, and beautiful, passionate Morwenna has clearly found a life without him. Can he win back the wife who gave him a reason to survive his ordeal? Or will the woman who haunts his every thought remain eternally out of reach?

Love lost and found? Or love lost forever?

Since hearing of her beloved husband's death, Morwenna

Nash has been mired in grief. After five bleak years without him, she must summon every ounce of courage and determination to become a Dashing Widow and rejoin the social whirl. She owes it to her young daughter to break free of old sorrow and find a new purpose in life, even if that means accepting a loveless marriage.

It's a miracle when Robert returns from the grave, and despite the awkward circumstances of his arrival, she's overjoyed that her husband has come back to her at last. But after years of suffering, he's not the handsome, laughing charmer she remembers. Instead he's a grim shadow of his former dashing self. He can't hide how much he still wants her—but does passion equal love?

Can Morwenna and Robert bridge the chasm of absence, suffering and mistrust, and find their way back to each other?

LORD GARSON'S BRIDE

(The Dashing Widows Book 7)

Lord Garson's dilemma.

Hugh Rutherford, Lord Garson, loved and lost when his fiancée returned to the husband she'd believed drowned. In the three years since, Garson has come to loathe his notoriety as London's most famous rejected suitor. It's high time to find a bride, a level-headed, well-bred lady who will accept a loveless marriage and cause no trouble. Luckily he has just the candidate in mind.

A marriage of convenience…

When Lady Jane Norris receives an unexpected proposal from her childhood friend Lord Garson, marriage to the handsome baron rescues her from a grim future. At twenty-eight, Jane is on the shelf and under no illusions about her attractions. With her father's death, she's lost her home and faces life as an impecunious spinster. While she's aware

Garson will never love again, they have friendship and goodwill to build upon. What can possibly go wrong?

…becomes very inconvenient indeed.

From the first, things don't go to plan, not least because Garson soon finds himself in thrall to his surprisingly intriguing bride. A union grounded in duty veers toward obsession. And when the Dashing Widows take Jane in hand and transform her into the toast of London, Garson isn't the only man to notice his wife's beauty and charm. He's known Jane all her life, but suddenly she's a dazzling stranger. This isn't the uncomplicated, pragmatic match he signed up for. When Jane defies the final taboo and asks for his love, her impossible demand threatens to blast this convenient marriage to oblivion.

Once the dust settles, will Lord Garson still be the man who can only love once?